3-00
(5)

CW00525413

BBP

CERTIFICATE OF AUTHENTICITY

Lochlaber Glen Trilogy

Book 1

Glen Rowan

This Limited Edition Hardcopy
is no. ...094... of 500 only

Signature *Anne L MacDonell*

Anne L. MacDonell

Lochaber Glen Trilogy

GLEN ROWAN

Lochaber Glen Trilogy

GLEN ROWAN

ANNE L. MacDONELL

First published in 2021 by Battlebridge Press, Ireland

Cataloguing in Publication Data is available from the British Library

Paperback ISBN: 978-1-7399171-0-4
Hardback ISBN: 978-1-7399171-1-1

Audiobook, narrated by the author, is available to download from
www.lochaberglen.com

Structural & Developmental Editor: Brian Connolly, County
Roscommon, Ireland
Typesetting and copy-editing: Paula Elmore, County Westmeath,
Ireland
Cover design by Walsh Colour Print, Castleisland, County Kerry,
Ireland
Public Relations and Marketing Consultant: Ivana Jokic, Dublin,
Ireland
Printed and bound by Walsh Colour Print, Castleisland, County
Kerry, Ireland

www.battlebridgepress@yahoo.com

About the Author

Anne L. MacDonell lives in the northwest of Ireland, but is a native of Fort William, Lochaber in the Scottish Highlands. Secretarial training led to her joining a company where she eventually became a director and company secretary. In her spare time, she took a degree in social science and had a career for many years as a probation officer in Greater London. This work gave her a great insight into the different ways people cope with life's challenges.

She is a multi-award winning short story writer. *The Lochaber Glen Trilogy* is her first series of novels. These were inspired because she often wondered how her own ancestors had lived and survived throughout the ages, but especially during the eighteenth century, the time of Bonnie Prince Charlie and the Jacobite Rebellion. A long gestation period and twenty years of research are the basis of these works.

ACKNOWLEDGMENTS

I WISH TO EXPRESS MY heartfelt gratitude to Mary Gallagher, Roscommon, Ireland, who played a major role in getting my work developed and completed, and all the people who got involved in the manuscript and gave constructive feedback, sometimes negative, sometimes positive but all genuine in their efforts to help me in their own way to construct this trilogy that I hope you enjoy.

Sister Frances Connochie, Glasgow; Helen Bally, La-Tour-de-Peilz, Switzerland; Renata Lange, Roscommon, Ireland; Sean & Carol McKay, Leitrim, Ireland; Kenny MacIntosh, Spean Bridge, Scotland; John Alistair MacDonell, Spean Bridge, Scotland; Orla Kelly, Reading Room, Leitrim, Ireland; Duncan MacPherson, Inverness, Scotland; Peggy Fleming, Roscommon, Ireland; staff and historians of West Highland Museum, Fort William, Scotland.

And a special thanks to the staff in Tesco, together with my friends in the Market Yard, in Carrick-on-Shannon, and also at the Ardcarne Centre, Roscommon, Ireland for their encouragement and their constant support during my journey.

PREFACE

S ET IN THE RUGGED beauty of the Scottish Highlands, with the famous Loch Ness in the north of the 'Great Glen', and Ben Nevis, the highest mountain of the British Isles, at the other end, this story reflects how the author imagines her ancestors lived their lives in Lochaber during the eighteenth century.

Their adventures, romances, dramas, feuds and battles are woven together to show how they struggled and survived at the time of the Jacobite rebellion, which was an attempt to install Bonnie Prince Charlie as the rightful King of Scotland and England and to topple King George ll.

While historical background events are accurate, this book is a work of fiction, based on stories handed down the generations, many years of research and the writer's own imagination.

Many who read this story are here today because their ancestors survived during these harsh times. In this book we meet: the spirited Sarah, aged thirteen; her courageous brother Ian Og, aged eleven; their uncle Angus, an illegal whisky distiller; their cousin Alistair Glic, a courier for the rebel army of Jacobites; 'The Frenchman', a double agent; MacCannie and his sons, trouble-making cattle rustlers; Granny Morag, a wise old healer who holds the family together, and many more interesting characters.

CHAPTER 1

Fort William, 1740

'DON'T BE LONG WITH THAT.' Sarah's clear young voice echoed sharply in all corners of the brew-house yard. Angus stopped. Although he was far bigger than his young niece, there was no ignoring Sarah as she waited beside the unladen pack horse, as compact and sturdy as the beast itself. Yet, under her shift and plaid there was a promise of future beauty. Two long untidy black plaits framed an oval face not yet mature, but now frowning with determination.

The loose assortment of baskets on Angus's back creaked as the big man turned to face her. He rarely needed to raise his voice. Men listened to him, but like many others, he was cautious with the words he spoke to womenfolk. They saw life in a different way and it was better to humour them, even if, like Sarah, they were only thirteen years old.

'I'll not be long.' He gave an apologetic half smile. 'These are the last of the baskets and I'll have to talk to Mr Gray and take a sup of ale as we sort out the payment. You could find Pepper somewhere to graze, and then take a look at the town. Maybe you'd like to look at that three-masted galleon which anchored in the loch this morning?'

A careful observer might have noticed that the leather strap was starting to bite into his forehead and small beads of sweat were forming, but Angus gave no other sign of discomfort. He made and sold his own baskets, and was commonly known as Angus 'Sticks' Mackintosh.

'Oh yes!' said Ian Og. Younger and slighter than his sister, with unruly black hair and dark eyebrows, there was no mistaking the family likeness. He would not be tall like his uncle Angus, but would fill out to become a strong reliable fighting man like his father, and Ian Mor, the grandfather he was named after. Now, he was just an eager boy whose eyes had been constantly drawn to the anchored ship since he first saw it on their way into the town.

Sarah was not so easily diverted. 'We're thirsty,' she said. 'We can stop for ale too.'

'Ah but pet,' said the sweating Angus, 'The ale house is for the soldiers. Your Mamma wouldn't like it.' After a moment he added, 'and your Dadda would kill me. No, you go and get a sup at the well by the parade ground, and have a look around the town till it's time to get down to your Auntie Kate's. It's business here.'

Sarah knew when to retreat. 'All right,' she agreed grudgingly. 'Maybe we'll go and have a look around.'

'And we'll see the ship too!' Ian Og added.

'Aye ... you'll see the ship as well. Get back here in

two, maybe three rosary lengths. Mind you don't go talking to any of those redcoats.' The wicker mass with Angus underneath turned towards the alehouse door, and they heard him mumble, 'They eat children.'

'Will you stop that?' Sarah said witheringly, halting her uncle once again although he didn't turn in case they would see the grin on his face. 'Really, Uncle Angus. You know that we're nearly grown up now. Ian Og is eleven and I'm thirteen. We haven't been children for some time, so you don't need to frighten us with stories.'

'Aye,' said her uncle thoughtfully. 'Where did the time go?' He put his hands up to ease the strain on the strap, and to wipe away the sweat. The load was weighing heavily and he started to move forward again. 'Well, off you go and maybe take a look at the street if you like. Don't go far. I know you've both got a few words of Scots but DON'T talk to the soldiers. Only a few have any Gaelic. Some of them have the French, but mostly it's only the Scots they have.' He said it disparagingly, paused for a moment to gauge the size of the low door before adding quietly, 'and the rest are just Campbell of Argyll's spies.'

He would have shaken his head sorrowfully, but the wide leather strap held firm and reminded him that there were four heavy gallons of untaxed whisky hidden under the baskets on his back. Carefully, he bent low and walked ahead. The creaking wickerwork, whisky and Uncle Angus disappeared into the brew house. Sarah and Ian Og stood for a moment. Despite Sarah's veneer of grown-up assurance, she was awed by the size of the garrison town before them.

Fort William dominated the town although the inside of the fort was mostly hidden, but it was still possible to see the tops of two long buildings with rows of neat windows, and several large houses which Uncle Angus said sheltered troops, horses and equipment. The gatehouse alone would have space for everyone from her own Glen Rowan, with room to spare. From the walls, black-mouthed cannon menaced the surrounding area, and the clutter of houses beyond. Angus said it was named after William II, known to many as William of Orange.

Having tied Pepper as instructed beside a patch of grass, they were free to explore. Around the front of the alehouse, on either side of the new road, there were houses in both directions. They were similar to the stone crofts up in Glen Rowan, except there were so many of them and all huddled together. The black waters of Loch Linnhe shivered as a cold wind blew up from the west. Sarah drew her plaid up around her shoulders.

Two soldiers hurried awkwardly along the road from the fort. One of them was tall and lean and the other was shorter and had a bit of a belly. They were too busy holding onto a ragged-looking boy wriggling between them to take heed of wide-eyed country children. Sarah watched the grim-faced men in awed silence, and Ian Og's normal exuberance was curbed until the trio ducked between two houses and went out of sight.

Curiosity would have caused them to follow cautiously, but an unearthly growling from the far end of the town stopped them in their tracks.

'Look at that!' Ian Og pulled at Sarah to make sure she was watching, but the noise would have wakened the dead. A wagon was slowly lumbering eastward towards the big wooden gates of the Fort. The wagoner sat atop the load, reins loosely draped around the fingers of one hand. He wore the same faded uniform as the two soldiers with the boy.

Locals would have identified the wagon as belonging to General Handasyd's regiment. A short clay pipe clamped between the wagoner's teeth puffed smoke in wheezy bursts, until he withdrew it long enough to hawk noisily and send a gobbet of brown spit arching to the ground. He appeared oblivious to the attention his equipment drew.

Every turn of the great wooden slab wheels provoked tortured squeals from the laden contraption. Two patient horses trudged in front, not small wiry garrons like those from the hills, but mighty creatures, nearly as great as the load they pulled. Walking leisurely beside them, with a proprietorial hand on the leather harness, was another smoke-belching soldier who occasionally spoke encouraging words to his charges.

Up in the glen, where wheels were used only to spin wool and linen, Sarah had never seen such an amazing sight. On the rough drove roads and mountain tracks, a travois-poled sledge was the only means of carrying loads too large for a horse's back. For several minutes she and her brother watched in awe the wagon's groaning progression towards the fort, until Ian Og remembered his goal.

'C'mon,' he said excitedly. 'Let's get down to the shore and see that ship.' They turned their backs to the noise and began to look for the path down to the loch.

As they passed people, the two nudged each other and pointed out strange garments and odd uniforms. In the glen, the usual clothing was the checked plaid, gathered around the waist in a double fold, or partly drawn up over the shoulders. Men also carried swords and dirks when necessary. The linen shirt with its many folds was rarer there, except for special occasions. However, here in the town no swords or dirks were visible. For twenty-five years the highlanders had not been allowed to carry weapons, but no doubt more than one armpit was shielding a knife (*sgian achlais*).

For the two country youngsters, it was much more interesting to look at tall men in breeches and buckled shoes, or women in dresses, wearing jackets to keep out the wind. Keppoch the Chief and his family sometimes wore these lowland clothes, but it was a rare sight in remote glens.

They came to a group of idlers watching four men carefully moving large logs onto the walls of a new building. There was plenty of conflicting advice in Scots and Gaelic as to the best means of attaching the ropes and levering the logs into place. Behind the noisy knot of spectators, two men in tandem patiently plied a double-handled saw, back and forward, swift and fluid, in rolling rhythm. Each completed piece of timber was laid neatly beside its fellow and the next begun with hardly a pause.

As they watched, the two became aware of a distinctive odour. Ian Og wrinkled his nose. Somewhere close, but out of sight, was a midden. With the odour came the sound of contented hens clucking as they scratched at the fresh manure.

It was as familiar as an old friend and Sarah began to realise that perhaps Maryburgh wasn't altogether such a strange place. She was getting used to the number of houses. Some here had rush thatch, but all used sturdy heather ropes weighted with stones to hold them firm against harsh winds blowing up the loch. They weren't so different from her home up in Glen Rowan, with its low walls and turf sod roof.

Several houses were joined end to end, runrig fashion. There was space between some of them where muddy paths led down to the water, and by the time Sarah remembered this was what they were looking for, Ian Og was already making his way between two of the houses. She began to run to catch up with him, but he heard her and with a laugh increased his pace to keep ahead.

'I'll race you,' he yelled over his shoulder and with great strides they rushed pell-mell down the brae.

A sudden cry of protest brought them both to a halt. There was a sickening dull thump of fist meeting flesh. No protest this time. Turning they saw the two soldiers they'd seen earlier, now standing beside an outcrop of rock. One held their young prisoner upright, while the other was pulling back a great fist to deliver another mighty wallop.

Before Ian Og could stop her, Sarah darted forward and grabbed the raised arm.

'You'll kill him!' she yelled in Gaelic.

The strength of the girl would not have been enough to stay the ham fist of Private Leonard Dickens, Lenny to his familiars, but the touch startled him. Glazed eyes turned to look at her. He belched and an acrid cloud of stale alcohol filled the air. Sarah stumbled back in disgust.

'*Well, well.*' The Scots voice was too thin and sneery to match the great fatness of him. '*A kitten and a mouse.*' He threw back his head in a scornful mirthless laugh and his great belly wobbled. '*Maybe they've come to rescue you boy, I'd say.*'

It was a temptation too great for a raging Sarah to resist. Ian Og saw what was to come and stood motionless. With a ferocity that outmatched her diminutive size, Sarah brought up a closed fist and drove it into the bulging belly. Surprise magnified the assault, and there was only a slight delay before an evening's spirits and a morning's generous top-up of ale began to revolt. The bully stood erect for a moment, before clutching his midriff and doubling over. Like a stream in full flow, slimy vomit gushed over the stones, narrowly missing brother and sister.

After his momentary stillness Ian Og took his cue and kicked the other soldier hard on the shin. It produced a gratifying groan, but there was no time to watch the man topple, as the young pair grabbed the hapless prisoner and dragged him away, slipping and sliding on the trail of vomit. Scrambling awkwardly, they rounded some rocks and hauled their prize down onto the grassy strip beside the stony shore.

Leaden feet pounded behind them. With hardly a nod to each other, the two continued to haul the boy out across the black crust of the high-tide line, and down the pebble incline, feet crunching loudly until they reached the damp lower line of seaweed. Here they stopped in the shelter of another great mound of black rock, to catch their breath and assess their pursuers.

The two men didn't follow them onto the stones. Instead they stood on the grassy path watching their quarry. The fugitives would have to leave the shore sometime. The tide was already on the turn and would climb steadily, bringing fronds of dead seaweed and little crab shells to join other detritus at the high-water mark. Biding their time would ensure their prisoner would be forced back into their custody.

'What now?' gasped Ian Og.

'Let me think.' Sarah shook her head to clear her mind.

'We can't stay here all day.'

'I know!' she snapped. 'But we can't just leave him.'

The ragged boy had been winded and was now coming to life again, and as she was speaking he started to struggle.

'*Let me go!*' he shouted in Scots and wrenched himself free from his two startled rescuers. He tried to run along the edge of the rock towards the water, but his recent beating took its toll, and within a few steps he stopped and took a look around him.

'*Where are they?*' he asked.

Sarah pointed to where the men stood watching.

The boy's shoulders drooped and tears of despair welled up in his eyes. '*They'll kill me this time.*'

Sarah didn't know the words, but the meaning was clear.

'They've not got you yet.' Her tone was matter-of-fact. 'I wonder what you did to them.'

'They … bad men,' the boy had found some Gaelic. 'Bad men steal. Want me steal. Think I tell.' His shoulders sagged even further and he sighed.

While they were speaking under the baleful gaze of the two men, two small fishing vessels approached on the waves behind them and drew towards the little jetty below the cluster of houses.

One of the fishermen sounded three blasts with a curved ram's horn, before jumping onto the wooden planking and securing his boat. It must have been a signal because women soon gathered, chatting together. Occasional bursts of laughter could be heard.

Ian Og and Sarah grinned at each other. By now the boy had recovered somewhat and was fully conscious. He tried to stagger forward by himself, but stumbled awkwardly, and then willingly put up his arms to take the assistance offered.

The town jetty was out of view of the soldiers on the grassy path, so although they heard the horn and knew people were gathering, they were not too concerned. So long as the boy was on the shore there was no way for him to escape.

'*I told you we should have taken him straight to the fort,*' whined Ash as he rubbed his smarting shin. '*It'll take ages to get him now.*'

'*Damn the boy,*' said his friend. '*I want that girl. I'll soon teach her a lesson she'll never forget. Maybe leave something for you, Ash.*'

Dickens began to walk along the track. It was only then he saw the large crowd gathered at the boats. '*Damn! We'll have to bide our time.*'

For Sarah and Ian Og, the sound of the raucous women was a relief, but their new friend remained alert. Cooped up in the fort most of the time, he knew that these people were the enemy, but with Nemesis standing on the grassy path, cackling hags were definitely a lesser evil.

The folk at the jetty were too concerned with the fishermen to take notice of three young ones moving among the crowd. The women carefully inspected the catch, turning it over. It was selling quickly. The older fisherman spoke only when commerce required it, but the younger good-natured one fielded all the mocking comments.

'That herring is so fresh it would nearly tell you itself,' he assured one matron as he bent down to put the fish into the reed matting she'd brought. For younger women he was more forward. 'A fine mackerel, it would nearly feed two, if there were to be two at the table.' His mousey brown curls quivered as he winked cheekily, and was rewarded with giggles.

One of the women called out, 'Watch that one.' The speaker was nearly toothless, with unkempt hair that framed a big cheerful face. 'He'll break your heart like he's broken many another.' She shook her head and turned to her friend. 'What are the youngsters coming to nowadays? We were never as bold as that!' She raised her voice. 'Give me those three fat herrings, young Alistair. Put them in these docken leaves.'

The fish were handed over and payment taken, but that was not all. No one saw the young fisherman accept a folded note of paper from the woman at the same time.

'Thank you, Mistress MacDee.' He spoke with exaggerated gallantry. 'Your custom is always valued, even if your man would be too jealous to find room for me at your table. I'll have to rely on some of these fine girls here.' Brown eyes sparkled as he looked down at Sarah. 'Maybe this girl would take me with her when she brings my fish home to her mother.' Although Sarah was still keeping an eye on the two soldiers, she felt there was something familiar about the fisherman and smiled shyly. Ian Og was more concerned that the two men were edging closer along the jetty and gave his sister a hefty push to try and encourage her to move out beyond the crowd. Unfortunately, she misinterpreted his action and shifted further along the jetty.

They would be safe while the crowd was gathered, but already women were leaving and soon the three would be visible to those pitiless eyes. The older fisherman had sold all his catch and was already settling his oars in the water to pull away from the jetty.

The other boat was still there and in an effort to hide for a little longer, Sarah climbed down into it and was quickly joined by Ian Og and the boy, whose name they now knew was Peter. They pressed themselves closely against the wooden planking at the stern of the little boat. They hoped the men would think they had moved further along the pebbly shore, to where there were more big rocks to shelter behind.

The three eyed each other fearfully and shrank even smaller when they heard the sound of running feet and shouts from the town above. They didn't see the young fisherman swiftly grab up his coins, and run to the edge of the jetty, tug sharply at the rope end and unhitch the boat. When he jumped aboard, he narrowly missed Ian Og. Shocked by the sight of three youngsters on board, he knew this was not the time for questions.

He sat down and quickly settled the oars between their pegs and started rowing. The oars bit firmly into the water and the little craft spurted away from the jetty and the three breathless pursuing redcoat musket-men.

CHAPTER 2

THERE WAS A DULL THUD. The cackling on the shore hushed for a moment, before 'plop!' The ball spent itself several yards from the boat, and then the muted voices rose again. The dripping oars did not falter, rising and falling in tandem, pulling the craft further away from the shore.

The next crack was hardly audible and the splash of the ball was no closer. After the sound of the third shot Ian Og stretched his neck to peep over the gunwale. Suddenly there was a screech. One of the women on the shore shouted, 'Look, a wee boy!' The cry was taken up by others, and the outnumbered soldiers reluctantly lowered their weapons.

Peter and Sarah slowly raised their heads. More screeching could be heard, but the words were lost as the boat pulled even further away. Soon the only sounds were of wavelets gently slapping against the sides, and oars cutting evenly into slate grey water. Mesmerised, the stowaways watched the shore receding.

'Where did you three appear from?' asked the fisherman.

Ian Og scrambled around to inspect their saviour, and the injured Peter followed, but Sarah found herself tongue tied. They were taking a great chance being in this boat with a complete stranger, however open and cheerful the face. It may have been twenty-five years since the rebellion in 1715, when the Earl of Mar raised the Old Pretender's standard at Braemar, but deep passions still simmered in many a breast. It took a moment for her to gather the courage to slowly turn around and take a good look at their benefactor.

He appeared to be unfazed by their presence. For Sarah, there was something strangely familiar about him. She guessed he was about eighteen or nineteen. Several little curls roamed free around his ears, but most of his brown hair was tied neatly back. Up in the glen, if neatness were required, fingers did the job well enough. Only Granny Morag possessed a horn comb, which Granddad had patiently made when he was wooing her. It was used by the women for great occasions. The fisherman's beard too was shorter than the Highland youngsters were used to.

'We were hiding.' Ian Og was the first to find a voice.

'Who were you hiding from?' It was a simple question, but again, for Sarah, there was something about his voice that confused her. It was both familiar and strange.

Ian Og, however, didn't hesitate. He liked the open, cheerful face of the man and told of seeing the two men bullying Peter, and how Sarah had given the fat one an almighty punch, which had allowed them to take their captive and run off. He added that Peter must get back into the fort.

Alistair turned to Peter and asked '*Why were they beating you?*' For a moment the boy didn't recognise his own tongue. Tears began to brim at the corners of his eyes.

'*They were stealing.*' The voice quavered with the effort of not crying. '*They were seen. Not just by me,*' he explained. '*Colonel Campbell set a trap for them, but they knew someone was watching. They thought it was me.*' He made a great sniff to try and clear his nose and carried on. '*When the sergeant sent me into the town this morning to help with the wagon, they grabbed me outside the gate.*' He sniffed again as a fresh bout of tears threatened to well up. '*I think they mean to kill me. There's talk of local rebels and they'd put the blame on them.*'

'Bastards!' the fisherman reverted to Gaelic.

'What did Peter say?' Sarah's curiosity loosened her tongue. 'I didn't understand much of it.'

The oars stopped. 'They hit him very hard. They want him dead.' Alistair shook his head. 'And they'll put the blame on us now.'

'Put the blame on us?' Sarah was indignant. 'We rescued him.'

He nodded. 'You're right.'

She looked at the boy shivering beside her. 'He's hardly more than a wet rag and they were hitting him. It isn't right.'

Ian Og agreed, nodding vehemently. 'Yes. It was Sarah's big punch to the belly that did it.' A proud smile grew on his face at the memory.

'It must have been a mighty punch.' The fisherman's thoughtful look was replaced by a grin.

It was this expression on his face which made Sarah think that he didn't really believe what they were saying. Before the fire within her had time to flare up, Ian Og spoke. He too had noted the broad smile.

'It was,' he insisted. 'And he boaked right there and then, everywhere.'

'Then Ian Og felled the other man with a kick on his leg.' Sarah felt it was only fair to give credit where it was due. This brought an even broader smile to the fisherman's face, as he lowered the oars and started to row again. The sparkle in his eyes would have lit up a darkened room. The irritation within Sarah started to boil over. With tightening jaw, she prepared to give this smiling stranger a harsh dressing-down, but with a chortle Alistair forestalled her.

'I'd have expected no less from a daughter and son of Duncan Ban and Mary MacDonell of Glen Rowan. With an uncle like your Angus, only the mightiest punch and the heartiest kick would have sufficed.' He couldn't contain a great gust of laughter.

There was a startled pause. 'Of course' breathed an astonished Sarah.

'It must be *fisniche faisniche*,' said Ian Og. 'You have the second sight.'

'No. No,' said Sarah. 'You're Alistair. Of course. Alistair Glic! Ian Og, it's Alistair, Cousin Alistair!' she beamed. 'I was only a wee girl when you were with us. Your Mammy was having a baby.'

'Yes, yes,' Alistair said, his eyes laughing. 'And I know that Angus Sticks is coming to Maryburgh this day, and he is bringing Sarah and Ian Og to help their Auntie Kate Cameron with the birth of her baby.'

Ian Og's face dissolved into a huge grin, and he began to pump Alistair's arm, while Peter with his few words of Gaelic tried to understand what was going on. When Sarah launched herself forward and enthusiastically hugged her cousin, the boat began to wobble. Fortunately Peter had the sense to grab hold of an oar that was dangerously close to falling overboard, and he prayed that the joyous reunion would not end with everyone in the water.

They were getting closer to the big ship anchored offshore in the loch. The stern of *The Leopard* loomed. It was like the wall of a steep cliff, with three glazed windows near the top. Beyond that was a tangle of ropes and pulleys. Small details thrust themselves into Sarah's vision: brown slime at the waterline; smeared pitch on the ship's side; flaked gilding around the many paned windows on the stern and a damp smell.

'*Ahoy!*' A shout from above rang out.

'Quiet!' Alistair hissed, his glance encompassing his passengers. 'Sit up, quickly.'

There was relief in uncurling from the fish-scaled bottom of the boat. As the wind blew around them, Peter and Sarah hunched themselves against the cold, but Ian Og greedily feasted his eyes upon every detail of this wondrous ship alongside. Each rope and spar was engraving itself on his mind, and he smiled with delight.

Alistair rested his oars for a moment and yelled back. '*Ahoy!*'

A head appeared and spoke in Scots. '*What's happening over there in the town? We heard muskets.*'

'*Not sure.*' Alistair sounded leisurely as he quickly wrapped Mrs MacDee's scrap of paper around a small stone. '*I think there was a mad dog and the soldiers shot it, but we couldn't see.*'

'*Mad dogs, terrible things,*' said the watchkeeper. '*Anyone get bit?*'

'*No. I don't think so,*' answered Alistair, deftly tossing the missile through one of the open hatches, where his contact 'The Frenchman' was waiting. His mission accomplished, he grasped the oars and rowed back into view of the sailor above.

'I told these three I'd bring them out to take a look at you, but they're not used to the water.' He waved cheerily and continued rowing around the ship and its anchor line, keeping up a line of banter with any of the sailors who looked over the side.

While the other two remained rooted, Ian Og waved enthusiastically at several of the men who came to see what was happening. Too soon for him they were turning back towards the shore, with Alistair finally calling up to the watchkeeper.

'These two are looking a bit green. I'd better get them home.'

Peter thought Alistair was something of a wild-looking creature. His plaid was old, frayed and none too clean, wafting a strong smell of fish at every stroke of the oars. Only he understood the exchange between the ship and the fisherman and was relieved that they were returning to dry land. He was still very sore from his beating and although he could swim joyfully in the river on a sunny day, the very thought of a cold doggy-paddle to the shore made his bones ache. Even if he evaded the attention of lurking sea monsters, there were still two deadly men waiting to prevent him reaching the fort. Already he would miss the midday roll call. He gave a great sigh, resigning himself to whatever fate God Almighty decreed.

Familiar words rose in his mind. *'Who go to sea in ships, and in great waters trading be, within the deep these men God's works and his great wonders see.'* Unfortunately, the psalm continued, waxing lyrical about the sea *'with rolling waves aloft'*, that *'mount to heav'n, and then to the depths they do go down again.'* With stomach churning, he looked longingly towards the shore and *'To the haven He them brings which they desir'd to see.'*

Sarah was straining her eyes to see if the two soldiers were still there waiting for them. She prayed that Angus would be there too. He rarely lost his temper, and he would have every right to berate them for getting themselves so spectacularly into trouble, but if he wasn't there to protect them, there was no guessing what the two soldiers might do. She smiled wistfully, reassuring herself that Angus would be there. The soldiers would be no match for him.

Back in the little settlement, a knot of people had gathered at the top of the brae beside the jetty. It was unusual to hear musket fire in the town except at the fort's practice range. The arrival of Angus Sticks prompted a vigorous retelling of events by several witnesses, fingers pointing towards the rowing boat out in the loch for emphasis.

The fugitives were steadily cutting a slice through the water away from the anchored ship, and he had no difficulty recognising the two he was supposed to be looking after.

Others would not have interpreted his wry smile towards Mrs MacDee as anything other than a comment upon the thoughtlessness of the youth of the day.

'Oh Angus Sticks. It's you. What a thing?' She barged across, keeping an eye on the scene below. 'Imagine, the soldiers shooting at that nice Alistair Glic, and me only after getting my fish. What can he have done?'

'Don't you be worrying, Mrs MacDee.' The tone was confidently avuncular. 'He's a good lad. It'll just be some high jinks he's at. Nowadays, they'll accuse anyone with a boat of being up to some kind of mischief.' He stooped to put a comforting arm around her, and continued, 'so long as he sold you a fine fish, and you didn't pay too much good money for it?' There was a query within his words.

'Oh aye' and with a gummy grin she lifted up the docken leaves and unveiled the herrings under his nose. 'They are very fresh and sweet.' Holding them up she said, 'Look, feel that.'

Angus gingerly prodded the fish with a grubby forefinger, while his other hand unobtrusively accepted a folded slip of paper.

'Aye,' he said. 'They're fine herrings, but if he doesn't get those two back here, it'll be a fine mess too.' He took out his pipe from the hide sporran dangling at his belt and stuck it into the corner of his mouth, sucking thoughtfully. 'Why has he got them at all?'

'They were playing in the boat when he took off. They'll be safe enough.' With a start she looked at him. 'D'ye know them?'

'I'm afraid so.' The pipe gurgled as he spoke. 'It's Sarah and Ian Og.'

'Are they your sister's children?'

He nodded. 'Aye, but I don't know the third.'

'The woman over there said it was wee Peter, the kitchen lad from the fort. Nice fellow by all accounts, but what he'd be doing with Alistair, I can't imagine. Colonel Campbell won't like it. He doesn't like the staff mixing with local folk.'

Angus removed his pipe and gave it a purposeful shake to dislodge some spittle. 'I was to take Sarah and Ian Og down to their auntie at The Weaver's house in Achintore, but this has delayed things.' He paused for thought. 'I'll go and get my cousin Hamish to take them. He'll be at the forge. He's always there. Too much, I think, but his mother, you know, ever since …'

The rest was unsaid, but several eavesdroppers nodded in pensive agreement. Many highlanders had been killed over the years by the soldiers, but most of them honourably, in fair fights. Hamish's father had died ten years ago in a drunken brawl with soldiers from the fort. There was no honour in that for anyone, and a grieving Lizzie was left to bring up their four children without her man. One or two would have been willing to take his place had she let them, but she was a proud woman. She was determined that her children would eventually bring honour to the false memory of the scoundrel she'd wed.

'I hope you find her in a good mood.'

'It'll only be for a wee while, Mrs MacDee.' Angus wasn't too confident and to reassure himself he added, 'She won't mind.'

'Aye,' the woman lied blatantly. 'I'm sure when she knows it's for your sister's family she won't mind.' At this thought her tone changed and she was much more sympathetic. 'And it must be nearly your sister's time up in Glen Rowan.' Heads bobbed among the women while they talked of babies and children and watched to see what would happen down on the loch.

'Aye,' Angus nodded distractedly. 'It's getting close for them both. Grannie Morag is up in the glen and she's sent Sarah to help down here. The girl's a gifted healer. She's been taught well. But gallivanting in boats! What can she be thinking of?'

The woman nodded, and then turned her head when someone in the crowd called out. 'Look! Look! They're on their way back' and hesitated before adding 'Maybe ...'

The boat's progress was being very carefully observed by others.

'What will we do, Lenny, if Peter gets away?' Ash looked enquiringly at his companion.

'We'll have to think of something,' replied Lenny.

'I would have thought it was convenient that he gets taken by rebels, led by Alistair Glic as well. There are plenty of witnesses, nothing to do with us.' Ash sounded hopeful.

'Aye, it would be handy for us if Peter was our only quarry, but MacCannie also wants Alistair Glic, and will reward us. There's some bad blood between them.' Dickens shook his head and began to walk faster. 'I know his son was killed when he tried to rustle cattle on Keppoch's land, and I think that Alistair Glic was the one who done the killing. He wants him caught with fresh blood on his hands. I don't think he cares whose blood it is. He can have Peter once we've finished with him.'

'He must be a rich thief when you're trying so hard, Dickens, to get into his good books.'

'Make no mistake, he's well connected with powerful friends. You have to admire him. He started with nothing, just like me.'

CHAPTER 3

Out on the loch, Sarah was full of confidence now that Alistair was at hand. 'Let's get back. We'll show them. The other soldiers will have gone and you'll be able to teach those bad men a lesson, and explain to Uncle Angus.'

'Just a minute … hold on.' It was difficult not to be caught up in Sarah's enthusiasm, but Alistair was well aware of the dangers he faced returning to town. 'Those soldiers aren't the only ones who may have an eye out for me. It'll do nobody any good if we get ourselves killed. I'm supposed to be heading down the loch, where I left my horse and goods this morning. I'll have to drop you off west of the town. You'll have no difficulty finding Angus from there. Peter can easily make his way around behind the houses and up to the fort.'

Sarah was taken aback a little by this apparent faint-heartedness, especially from someone whose exploits were a byword for bravery amongst the family. 'You can't just dump us, and so far from the fort. Those two bullies will be watching to see where we land.'

Ian Og chimed in. 'Peter wouldn't have a chance.'

Although he didn't understand all the words, the boy began to hunch up again. It was enough to melt a stone, and Alistair paused.

'Just a minute,' he said. 'Let me think.' He shipped the oars and allowed the boat to drift, bobbing like a cork in the shallow waves. 'Our meeting like this has made things worse for all of us. The sooner we go our separate ways the better.'

Despite the words, Sarah was quick to notice a softening in his tone. 'Well, it's true we can't stay here.' She was matter of fact. 'I suppose we're lucky there isn't a boat after us already. They're probably watching and waiting for us to return to the shore, so we'll have to think of something to confuse them, while we find a way to sneak Peter into the fort by a back door.'

'That's a thought,' said Alistair and addressed himself to Peter. '*Is there another way into that fort?*'

The boy shrugged his shoulders. He didn't know of any easy way in. '*Sometimes men climb the back wall when they miss the curfew.*'

'We can help Peter do that,' said Sarah excitedly when Alistair explained his words. The wall by the edge of the river had stones that were rougher than the ones facing the parade. They all knew it would be difficult, but it was possible.

The boy continued. '*They need someone inside with a rope, because it is very high for a man to climb.*' Dejectedly he looked down at the choppy wavelets and quietly added, '*And it's even higher for me.*'

'He doesn't sound too hopeful, Alistair.' Ian Og was trying to think of ways to climb high walls.

'No. He's not.' Alistair mused. 'But between us all we should think of something.' He looked towards the shore. It was too far to see if the soldiers or the crowd had dispersed. A gust of wind came up the loch from the west and the small craft swayed and shook. 'We definitely can't stay here.'

With renewed purpose he took the oars, settled each one onto its wooden peg, and turned the bow eastwards. As they passed the stone fort they all took a good look, to try and gauge where there might be footholds for a desperate lad to climb up.

When the boat approached the point where river met loch, the keel was jerked sideways by the strong current. There was a sharp intake of breath from Ian Og, and Sarah clamped her lips together determinedly. Peter grabbed the side strake nearest to him, jarring his side further and held on grimly.

Alistair's pace on the oars faltered, but he quickly recovered and manoeuvred towards the bank, where birch and willow trees overhung the water in a tangle of spring foliage. As the stem of the boat glided under the leafy canopy, Alistair drew his oars completely into the craft. He grabbed at branches above. 'Duck!' he said. Peter ignored the pain in his side and like the others, brought his head down.

Behind the greenery was a narrow channel of the river. Peter lifted his head up a little, and over the side he could see pebbles and sand under the water. There was a grinding noise each time the bottom of the boat scraped against stones, but there was just enough water to keep them afloat. Alistair gripped branches ahead and slowly drew them upstream.

A little further on, the line of trees was less dense. Riverbank and shore were becoming one. At Alistair's nodded command, Ian Og jumped out and looked around. Then he tied the boat to a birch sapling, and the others scrambled out. It was low ground and pretty marshy, but firm enough to hold even Alistair, if he chose his route carefully.

Although Peter managed to climb out of the boat without any help, he still looked very fragile.

'I'll give him a hand' volunteered Sarah. 'You two go and check ahead.'

From the shoreline, the sight of the mighty grey mountains rising almost vertically from the floor of the glen was spectacular, and served as a reminder to men of their own insignificance. Even the fort shrank against such a backdrop, but Alistair and Ian Og knew it would take ingenuity to find a way over the walls. At Alistair's signal to Sarah to bring Peter, the two made their way through the reeds and grassy tufts.

Inside the fort the soldiers sent to arrest Alistair Glic reported to the garrison commander that he appeared to have kidnapped some children, and in an effort to avoid capture had rowed up towards the mouth of the River Lochy and was lost to sight. Colonel Campbell was not a foolish man. He had information that Alistair was a Jacobite courier. It was highly unlikely that such a person would saddle himself with children, and take them for a jaunt out in the bay and around *The Leopard*.

Although four more men would be dispatched to try and apprehend him, he didn't think their mission would be successful. Sure enough, when the soldiers reached Lochyside they found tracks in all directions, and by the time they could find out where man and boat landed, there was little chance of guessing which route he might have taken, even if he were held back by children.

Dickens and Ash, in the meantime, were still following their quarry. Dickens walked briskly, but Ash was finding it difficult to keep up with his companion. '*Slow down.*' He called.

The ground was rough and they slowed to a halt. '*I can't walk too much further,*' wheezed Ash again. '*I'll start looking along the river's edge here. You go on ahead.*'

With a nasty smile, Dickens nodded to himself. '*We'll soon have that Peter.*' The grin widened to show several tobacco-stained teeth. He hawked from deep within his chest and spat fulsomely before adding. '*But there's a Highland lass and lad that need to get a lesson as well.*'

Not far ahead, their fugitives were at the River Nevis, which was fed from the cold dark mountains that towered above. It took the shortest distance across the flat plain to the loch, bounding carelessly over boulders, raising spray to hang in the air and catch the afternoon light. This was a more vigorous opponent than the meandering River Lochy, and they would need to take care not to be swept off their feet as they crossed.

Ian Og was carrying a coil of rope from the boat over his shoulder, and as they walked he stooped and broke off some green willow sticks and stuck them into his belt. 'We can use these like we do at home,' he muttered to himself.

Private Ash was still finding that walking through the ragged clumps of birch and willow was difficult, but with money at stake he urged himself onwards. Had he turned around and looked towards the fort itself, he might have seen his quarry, but he didn't. Instead, he caught sight of the boat under its leafy canopy.

There was an area of large boulders that formed a little island in the scrubland. It was a sheltered spot where he could watch the boat and the river. His leg throbbed and his mouth was as dry as a kiln. There was no sense in chasing shadows. He took off his jacket and sat down with his back resting on a sloping rock.

By this time he could feel quite a bump on his leg. After a struggle with his leggings it was possible to see the skin was already turning black. He cursed the brat who did it, and Peter, the cause of all the trouble. Rummaging in his pouch he found a lump of tobacco, and took a bite before he lay back. After chewing for a few minutes, he folded his jacket into a pillow and settled down to wait.

Back at the river, Peter sat in the shelter of a small rock while the others decided on the best means to cross the water. Peter had almost been kicked to death by the soldiers and he was in no fit state to try and cross the river unaided. The three highlanders had a discussion, and Sarah tied the middle of the rope around her own waist. Alistair and Ian Og went across carefully, each taking one end of the rope. 'C'mon Peter.' She clucked her tongue and signalled him to put his arms around her neck. As she hoisted him in a piggy-back position, he stifled a groan by gritting his teeth, as his pain got even worse.

Feeling each step with her toes, Sarah made her way into the rushing water. Alistair and Ian Og stood apart, each keeping his end of the rope firm, so that she might steady herself as the force of the river pulled against her. Gradually she was able get across and at last Peter was able to slide down onto dry land again.

'*I'm sorry,*' he said as his legs buckled under him. '*I'll never get over that wall.*'

Ian Og gave him a reassuring pat, and brought out

the bunch of willow rods he had been gathering along the way. 'We have an idea,' he said.

Alistair watched as Ian Og and Sarah broke the rods into lengths of about one foot and then with a twist, folded each one back on itself.

Between brother, sister and newly found cousin, it was decided that although Ian Og was undoubtedly the better climber, he should go back through the rushing river to keep watch for any soldiers. Sarah was to make the ascent of the wall. Older and heavier, her strength would be more solid than Ian Og's and better for the task ahead.

There wasn't much cover for the few yards between river and fort, only fresh spring growth. Colonel Campbell had strict rules for preventing surprise rebel attacks. Parties of unenthusiastic soldiers were sent out occasionally to thrash aimlessly at bushes or reeds which had the temerity to rise more than a foot or so from the ground around the walls. It was fortunate that the task wasn't seen as an urgent one, and there would be just enough spring greenery to hide the three of them from a cursory glance.

Peter told them that the wall was supposed to be patrolled at intervals, but Lochaber was a wet spot, and the soldiers on guard knew that the best way to avoid a soaking in driving rain was to keep under cover. Unless the old colonel was making an inspection, they only made full rounds of the walls at the beginning and end of their two-hour watch. Mostly they spent their time near the main gate looking at what was happening in the town, or watching cattle on the Cow Hill above it. On the eastern side of the parade ground, beside the new road, there was a cemetery and a rocky outcrop known as the Craigs. An army might try and shelter behind that, but there wasn't much heed paid to the narrow grassy strip beside the river, under the shadow of the fort's wall. That's where Peter and his new friends now stood, undetected.

All the willow wands having been cut and twisted, Sarah tucked them into her belt. She put the looped rope over her head and one arm, to prevent it getting in the way during the climb. With his back to the wall Alistair leaned forward and locked his fingers together. Sarah took hold of his shoulders, and lifted her foot to step onto his palms. Looking down she could see the pale skin on the inside of his wrists and became very aware of how physically close she was to this man, whom she'd only known as a child. Her nostrils were picking up the not-unpleasant smell of his body. Buried within the acrid odour of fish that had so nauseated Peter, there was the sharpness of salty new sweat and a tang of peat smoke.

The moment was gone before she had formed the thought, but the smell stayed in her nostrils as she put her weight and her trust into those hands. She dared not catch his eyes as he hoisted her upwards. 'Good girl,' he said encouragingly. 'We'll have a tale to tell when this is done.'

Standing on his shoulders with the wall only inches from her face, Sarah commended her spirit to God, made a sign of the cross and then took a good look at the stones beside her. There had been no hint this morning when she walked past the fort that only a couple of hours later she would be trying to storm its walls. Beneath her feet, Alistair was concerned she might be having second thoughts. 'Come on, Sarah,' he urged. 'Time to make a start.'

He appeared to have no questions about her ability,

so she took a deep breath to calm herself and sought the first handhold of the climb. Thinking only of the task, her mind cleared and without another qualm she hoisted herself from the comfort and safety of Alistair's shoulders, up onto the cold stone wall.

The stones were quite rough but she was able to grasp them at the corners. There were gaps between them into which a strong finger or a flexible toe could just fit. She didn't know how much experience or fitness the lad might have, but the springy willow twigs she lodged between the stones would give him the extra help he would need to get safely up the wall.

It was slow work, step up, hand up, rod placed, foot up, next hand up, and all the while the number of twisted rods in her belt dwindled until there were none left. She hoped they would be sufficient to do the job. Finally, with a desperate effort Sarah grabbed the edge of the parapet and hauled her upper body over the top. Lying on the edge of the wall with bruised fingers and cramped legs, the support beneath her was a great relief. There were sounds of activity, but no alarm. Slowly she glanced around her. There was no one nearby. She eased herself onto the wooden ledge around the inner wall, and crouched down to avoid being seen by anyone below.

Although this part of the wall did not have cannon, Peter said there were rings bolted to the wall near one of the openings, which Sarah soon found. One end of the rope went through a ring, so she gave it a good tug to make sure it would hold, and then dropped both ends outside the wall before crouching down again.

From a distance, Ian Og quietly breathed a sigh of relief. It was some months since they'd last raced up the open face of Craig Dhu. Sarah was a good climber, and even if he reached the top first, it would not be long before she would be sitting beside him looking down at the glen below. She obviously hadn't lost her skill.

He would have stayed and watched how Peter fared, but he heard a noise; voices upstream. He crouched into the reeds and then went to see who was coming. Colonel Campbell's soldiers were making their way towards the Nevis Ford. They didn't seem to think that the fugitives were in the area, and made no secret of their presence. Ian Og slowly began to retreat. It was unfortunate that the track he chose took him past the recumbent Private Ash.

The soldier could hardly believe his luck when Ian Og, oblivious to his presence, crept past the stony outcrop. Ash was a slovenly soldier but he was light on his feet. Quickly he rose, and picking up his jacket from the ground, he sneaked up behind the unsuspecting Ian Og. He threw the jacket over his head, and tied the sleeves around him, so that the boy was now blindfolded and pinioned.

'*I have ye now,*' he growled.

Young energy was no match for grim determination. With a strong grip, Ash took care that his quarry would not slip from his grasp. He delivered a smart punch through the jacket to hush the boy's protests. Dazed, the lad could offer no resistance. Ash raided the boy's sporran and found a long strip of linen, which made a fine gag. He removed the jacket and having gagged him, wrapped Ian Og's plaid around his head and arms, and tied it with his belt so that only bare buttocks and legs were visible. He cared little that he was adding indignity upon injury to his victim.

Back in the shadow of the fort's wall, Alistair was grateful the day was still dry. Wet walls would have made the task impossible. He helped Peter to remove his jacket and used it to pad the loop he'd formed at the end of the rope, and then brought it carefully over Peter's head and under his arms. The boy was conscious and willing, but still weak from his beating. Because of the injuries and soreness in his side, Sarah and Alistair agreed he couldn't just be hauled up like a sack, but must use his own hands and feet to take some of the weight. Alistair would hold the free end of the rope and be prepared to take the full strain if Peter fell, while Sarah would keep her end taut and guide him upwards.

Once again Alistair cupped his hands and Peter slowly climbed onto his shoulders, while Sarah braced herself above. Before he began his climb, the boy took a glance at the mountains, and then adjusted his position to face the large stones and seek the first of the willow rods. With a whispered 'Thank you' in Gaelic to Alistair, he began to climb.

His lips moved in prayer. *'I to the hills will lift mine eyes, from whence doth come mine aid. My safety cometh from the Lord, who heav'n and earth hath made.'*

The psalm helped to calm him, and carefully he sought out each hand- and foothold. Every inch he gained was hard won, and gradually the rope above him began to shorten. The words of the psalm were spoken quietly to the wall and although there were only two verses, he repeated them again and again. He was near the top of the wall when one of the willow rods slipped. It sprang out of its crevice and dropped.

Sarah, hands straining at the rope, was not able to see the progress of her charge, but felt the tension suddenly waver and instantly braced herself. Down below, Alistair had seen Peter falter and was already tightening his end of the rope. Peter would have fallen but the rope held him with a jerk. A low moan was wrung from him, but with determination he kicked his boot into the crack, and slowly continued while praying, *'The Lord shall keep thy soul; He shall preserve thee from all.'*

Sarah felt the rope slacken slightly and breathed a sigh of relief. She hoped that none of the soldiers within the fort would catch sight of her, until at least Peter was safely over the top. The last part of the climb seemed to take an age, although it was only a few minutes later that Peter's wan face appeared at the top of the wall.

Sarah dared not loosen her grasp of the rope until he was safely on the parapet, and then helped him onto the guards' walkway. Although Peter was nearly exhausted, he grasped Sarah gratefully by the hand, pumping it up and down in an effort to say what words could not express.

'Aye, aye,' she said reassuringly. 'Go on, good luck.' Then with a quick look over the wall, checking that the rope was still looped through the wall ring, she edged herself over and slowly began to climb back down.

As she descended, she dislodged any willow twigs that remained, so there would be no evidence of the climb. Her descent was steady and swift and her heart was pounding, but there was no sound of discovery. On the ground again, she let go one end of the rope to draw it through the far ring. Looking up she saw it snake its way down, and then from the top of the wall a small hand waved.

Down on the ground, Alistair whispered to Sarah with a big smile, 'You are a hero.' He clasped her in a generous hug, and then turned to pick up the rope. 'Time we were elsewhere.' Now the tone was businesslike. 'We'll leave the boat where it is. Someone will get it another time.'

With a last look around he asked. 'Will you be all right if I leave you now? I have to get my horse and report to Keppoch himself.'

After the exhilaration of the climb and Peter's safe return, Sarah wanted the feeling to last forever. 'You'll be going to Keppoch Castle, will you, up on the hill, between Glen Spean and Glen Roy? I've been there several times, when someone was getting married and all the Keppoch Clans came to celebrate. It's big, isn't it?'

'Oh yes,' said Alistair. 'You can see for miles around up there.' But he realised that he could not let himself be distracted by this bonnie young cousin while he had messages for Keppoch that could not wait. 'I must leave you now. If you meet any soldiers, you can always say that you were kidnapped and put ashore.'

For Sarah, it didn't seem fair that the person with whom she had just shared this great adventure was acting as if nothing had happened. It was as if he hadn't felt any of the excitement and danger, and the whole matter had just been a short delay in his day. He would forget all about it as soon as he was out of sight. She wanted to stand tall and hit him, so that the memory would not fade, but she knew there was no sense in that.

'I'd better go and get Ian Og and we'll cut back through the town to Mr Gray's alehouse,' she babbled, adding, 'At least Peter is safe.'

Alistair nodded. 'Peter is safe and I have to go. There is a meeting of the clan chiefs tonight, and I have to be there. I am meeting an important envoy tomorrow night at Kinlochmore.'

'He must be very important,' said Sarah, wishing to keep up the conversation.

'He is,' Alistair nodded. 'He's with the Jacobite Royal Scots troops and gathers information for the Prince. We call him "The Frenchman".'

Now that the moment to leave was upon him, Alistair found he was reluctant to leave this gallant girl and get on his journey, although he wouldn't have admitted as much to anyone. 'I must go now and get my horse before the soldiers find me. Give my love to your mother. She'll probably give you a row when you tell her what happened. I know I'll be for it when next I meet her.'

'I'll give her your love,' said Sarah. 'You'd better be off, and I'll go and get Ian Og.'

She stood for a while watching Alistair crouching as he ran from bush to bush. Then he disappeared over a wall. Sarah waited in case there might be another glimpse, but there wasn't. It was time to fetch Ian Og. Uncle Angus was going to give them a terrible telling-off, but she was sure he would understand when he heard their story.

This time, without Peter on her back and with plaid and shift tucked up, she was not troubled by the force of the river. Soon she was picking her way through the reeds and rushes towards Alistair's boat, whispering Ian Og's name as loudly as she dared, as she skirted the bushes and rocks.

A blackbird 'pinked' at her and clumsily fluttered away. Then all was quiet for a moment. From the water's edge a moorhen went 'poot'. There came a distant murmur of men's voices. Her heart beat faster for a moment, but it was only the soldiers on the road: confident, careless talk, short bursts of laughter. There was no sign of Ian Og.

Sadness and fear welled up inside her and she could not blink away the tears that gathered. She found it difficult to think clearly. First, she must get safely off the rough ground. As she moved through the reeds and rushes, she continued to call quietly around her, just in case she was wrong and Ian Og might hear, but the emptiness of the river plain told her with certainty that further searching would be fruitless. Ian Og was not there.

CHAPTER 4

Down in the ruins of Comyn's Castle, MacCannie was starting to break camp, when Dickens joined him and told him of the day's events. Despite Dickens's assessment of the man, MacCannie had been a reliable drover until the year the cattle prices fell very low. A whole community came close to starvation that winter, and he'd been hunted out of his home village in disgrace. Since then he had made his living by other means. More than one herd had been driven off by his men and sold to dealers who asked no questions.

In the Trossachs he became known as a dangerous man. The cattle drovers of Badenoch and Lochaber had fearsome reputations and guarded their own herds closely. Twice MacCannie was thwarted. The second time he'd been set upon by a band of MacDonells and one of his sons was killed. They were led by Alistair Glic, on whom MacCannie had sworn revenge.

When a small group of rich merchants and powerful landowners made it clear there would be profit for him if trouble arose among the Lochaber clans, MacCannie was a willing volunteer. It would serve both to increase his purse and settle a score that still rankled. Since then he had taken a great interest in gossip, whether in Gaelic or Scots. Sometimes in the rare hostelries that lay in the path of the herdsmen, he might be seen to put his hand into his pouch and buy a fill of whisky for a new acquaintance. By these means he slowly learned the ways of the Camerons and the MacDonells, and most particularly of Alistair Glic.

He knew of Alistair's planned rendezvous in Kinlochmore with 'The Frenchman'. It did not worry him that the young adventurer might be diverted: Alistair Glic could be relied upon to attend the meeting come hell or high water. For MacCannie, the question was whether Dickens and Ash would still be able to keep their part of the bargain.

He'd first met the two soldiers in the yard of Mr Gray's alehouse, where they were selling boots and cloth, later found to be missing from the storehouse at the fort. When their activities were discovered, they believed that it was Peter, the keen young kitchen boy, who had betrayed them. Neither Dickens nor Ash liked him. They teased him about his piety, the Bible and the psalms he quoted, chapter and verse. When MacCannie suggested kidnapping as a means to remove him, and offered money to bring the boy to him, the soldiers jumped at the chance.

MacCannie and Dickens set off to find Ash when they met Sergeant Beech with several of his soldiers. As MacCannie waved cheerily to the men, quietly he said to Dickens, *'Get rid of them. I'll go and take a look for Ash and he'd better have something for me.'*

Emphasising a painful looking limp, Dickens approached the sergeant. *'I'm glad to see you!'* he said. *'I've done something to my ankle.'* He gratefully took the help of two of the soldiers and began earnestly to question the others about the search. While they were chatting, the men spotted Ash in the distance and headed towards him.

Realising that the soldiers were coming his way, Ash tucked Ian Og behind some boulders, pulled grass and heather over him and then moved quickly towards the men.

For him, any search party was likely to prove inconvenient. While he might have received praise for catching a rebel, even a small one, there would have been questions about why he didn't call them over to help. No one in the fort would quarrel with his decision to bind the rebel lad so tightly or hit him so hard, but secrecy was likely to raise suspicion, especially after the death of his last prisoner. Martial law might still be in force, but soldiers no longer had free rein for all their actions.

MacCannie called out to the soldiers. *'Any sign of the rebels?'*

Sergeant Beech answered. *'It's only Ash. He's a bit of a rebel, but not what we're looking for.'*

The very slight nod by Ash was interpreted by MacCannie as success. He smiled broadly in response. *'Ah well, nothing to be found here.'*

'Let's get back before that rain reaches us,' said Dickens.

The men turned to Beech for his assent, and smiled when he nodded.

Dickens put out his arm. *'Ash, can you give me a hand? I might take a bit of time.'* As all the soldiers knew both men well, none were likely to assist either willingly.

'*Any luck?*' MacCannie asked Ash when the other soldiers were out of earshot

'*Oh yes, he nearly tripped over me.*'

'*Peter?*'

'*No. It wasn't Peter. It was the rebel lad. He was with Alistair Glic in the boat. He won't go far unless someone finds him.*'

'*Sounds like a job for the lurchers.*' With a slight nod to both of them, MacCannie took his leave.

'*I wonder what happened to the girl,*' Dickens mused.

'*I definitely didn't see her,*' Ash responded quickly.

MacCannie was pleased. His faith in the two soldiers had paid off, and the day was going as planned. Finding the boy among the low scrubland would be easy. A sharp pair of eyes accustomed to spotting odd shapes and colours among rocks and vegetation saved tired feet from walking many a barren mile. The lurchers bounded enthusiastically across the ground, barking.

Ian Og struggled to compose his thoughts after the rapidly changing events of the day. One moment he was looking forward to seeing the big new ship in the harbour, and the next he was a prisoner. When Ash left him, he tried to collect his thoughts. He lay gagged and trussed in his own plaid, and his head throbbed. He couldn't believe what was happening. Blood was oozing from his nose, and his cheek felt as if it were twice its usual size. He could hear voices, but they weren't talking Gaelic and they were moving away.

He kicked his legs and tried to yell, but the gag around his mouth did its work well. The effort only made his cheeks hurt more. He wondered what was going on. The soldiers would not mistake a boy of eleven for Alistair Glic. He could only imagine that they were going to question him about being on the boat, but tying him up so tightly and then leaving him didn't make any sense.

Ian Og's sense of outraged justice throbbed more than his bloody nose and swollen cheek. He'd not caused them any trouble. But then, remembering Sarah's great punch and his mighty kick, his heart sank: this had to be a cruel revenge. His best course was to get away as quickly as he could, but it was difficult to move while his ankles were bound so tightly. His captor knew his trade and extricating either leg was impossible without a hand to help. It was his own belt that bound his arms and wrists behind him, but he could feel a slight slackness, as though his abductor had been in a hurry to finish the work. He took a deep breath and strained again and again to free himself.

Light rain began to cool his naked lower body but the binding chafed his skin. He continued to try and work his way free. After a few minutes there was the panting sound of dogs running across the ground, and soon they were sniffing at him. He kept as still as he could before the animals bounded away, barking. His heart was pounding. There were more voices and his heart pounded faster.

'*Good boy, Hawk.*' A voice praised one of the dogs and Ian Og expected reassurance for himself, but there was none. Instead, the voice said, '*We've got him. It's the Highland boy. Gather him up and let's go.*'

Lifted like a sack of meal he was thrown over a broad shoulder, and although he threw his weight around to try and free himself, it had no effect. The man moved quickly through the scrubland, taking little notice of the wriggling burden except to hold him more firmly. Struggling seemed pointless. The man was big, nearly as large as Angus Sticks.

There was a distant shout. It sounded like an old woman. 'I see you … I see you.' The words came again. 'You bad men … I see you.'

Ian Og was dumped on the ground. *'I'll go and sort her out.'* It sounded as if the Goliath who carried him was keen to be rid of the irritation, but then came another voice.

'Not now, there's no time. We don't want to cause any unnecessary alarm.'

'But she's seen us, MacCannie!'

'Doing what?' The words held contempt. *'And besides, who's she going to tell? No, leave her.'*

It was the air of authority with which the words were spoken that told Ian Og that MacCannie must be the leader. By this time he knew there were three of them: Goliath, his carrier, whom they called Hugh; MacCannie, who was the leader; and his young nephew Ken, who was responsible for the dogs. While they were distracted by the old woman, Ian Og desperately tried to move his wrists. If he could only get himself free, he was sure he could outrun the men into the town or at least into some cover. But too soon he was hoisted back up over the same broad shoulder.

'Well, this is a lively one,' said Goliath, slapping him on his bare buttocks. *'Why don't we kill him here and be done with it? Dead meat's easier to carry.'* Ian Og hoped he had misunderstood the words, but MacCannie's reply left no doubt. *'We don't want him dead yet. It's blood we need.'*

'Let's get away. If anyone follows, they'll take a while working out which way we went.'

The casual way the men spoke was more chilling to Ian Og than anything that had happened so far. Whatever they were planning included his death, and that realisation robbed him of the strength to struggle any further for now.

The journey took on a timeless quality. In his desperation, Ian Og's mind drifted in and out of the present. There was no way he could escape while thrown carelessly over a broad shoulder. He resigned himself to his fate, but just for now. Opportunities to escape might be scarce and he would need to grasp his chance instantly.

Back at Maryburgh, by the time the last of the search party reached the outskirts of the town, Lenny Dickens was in good spirits. He wasn't a man to give up money lightly. Now he wouldn't need to return MacCannie's siller, and at least one of the two brats would receive his comeuppance. There was satisfaction in a job well done, and it would reassure MacCannie that if there were other jobs to be done, he would be the man.

'*You'll be all right now, won't you, Ash?*' Dickens asked. '*Maybe I'll take a look along the road for a while.*' He paused. '*It wouldn't do me any harm to get into the colonel's good books. Maybe the drovers have seen something. I'll go and ask.*'

'*Well, you please yourself,*' said Ash and carried on towards the town, and into another burst of rain, which was making its way up the loch from the west.

Near the road, hidden by boulders, Sarah was watching. She saw the fat bully there with the soldiers, and as they began to hasten towards the town, she watched him turn around and walk purposefully eastwards in the opposite direction.

Sarah would have been soaked had her clothing not been made with homespun linen and the oil-rich wool of hill sheep. The rain was cold on her face, but it wasn't that which caused a shiver. She pulled the plaid up to cover her hair. It was clear that something bad had happened to Ian Og.

Her common sense called for her to return to the town, find Angus and maybe learn that her brother was already with him, but the grey cloud in her heart could not be ignored. A smiling face with greenish-brown eyes came into her mind: it would have been a comfort to have Alistair with her, but even alone she must keep going.

The soldiers were out of sight before she emerged from her hiding place. There was little cover beside the road, so she stayed close to the scrub and bushes, ready to duck behind them if that vengeful man she was now following were to turn around.

Along the road, another youth was not so concerned to remain hidden. He didn't know exactly what was going on, but Angus Sticks had put his trust in him to find Sarah and Ian Og, and get them safely to their auntie at The Weaver's house down at Achintore beside Loch Linnhe.

The red-haired Hamish would have died rather than let his cousin down. Angus was one of the few people who stood up to Lizzie, his ambitious mother, and she trusted his advice. An unenthusiastic Hamish would have been sent to train as a lawyer three years ago had Angus not pointed out to her that this would have taken him away for months at a time. Even then, he was already spending much of his time at the forge, and if he were to be apprenticed to the blacksmith, Lizzie would become the mother of a worthy local tradesman, bringing security and comfort to her in her old age. For a woman who would never have admitted that her life had taken a distinct turn for the better the day her man died, this swung the argument and Hamish was allowed to follow the path he really wanted.

After searching the town, Hamish headed out towards the River Lochy, and met the soldiers on their way back. They were known to him and responded openly when he carelessly asked in passing about their efforts. He was heartened by their lack of success: Sarah and Ian Og were probably still with Alistair and should be safe with him, so he ran on.

The sight of a girl near the road ahead cheered him greatly. It looked as if his mission was accomplished. 'Sarah!' he called, and then again 'Sarah!' before stopping and bending over to catch his breath.

She stopped, ready to defend herself, but sighed with relief at the sight of this spotty red-haired Highland lad, panting in the middle of the road, rain mixing with sweat on his face. Then she was annoyed that she'd been so startled.

'Quiet!' she snapped in a harsh whisper. 'They might hear you.'

'Who might hear me?' Hamish immediately dropped his voice and turned his head but could see no one. 'Do you mean Ian Og?'

'No.' Sarah was scornful at the suggestion. 'Keep quiet,' she urged again, and then began to sob.

This was not what Hamish was expecting. He came closer and put his arm around her as he would have done to any of his sisters. 'It's all right, I'm here. Angus sent me to make sure you're all right.' He looked around. 'Ian Og … Where is he?'

'Quiet!' The word was less commanding as it emerged between snuffles. She pointed along the road. 'I don't know. I think the soldier ahead knows. We have to follow him.'

Hamish was a bit mystified. He was expecting to take a frightened lass and her brother under his wing, and lead them the last few miles to their auntie's house; but although she was distressed, Sarah had strength within her and he did not question her use of the word 'we'. Nor did he hesitate to follow as she moved forward to another clump of bushes.

After a few minutes, he whispered, 'Who are we following?'

Only when she felt sure that the soldier Dickens was far enough ahead did she answer. As she told Hamish some of the day's events, he marvelled at this determined girl with wet wisps of black hair escaping from the cover of her plaid. She might be only as tall as his shoulder, but she was full of spirit, and Hamish MacNeil thought he had never seen anyone so fine.

If Sarah was asked beforehand, she would not have picked this red-haired, gangly youth to accompany her in her quest to find Ian Og, but there was kindness within him which, despite her distress, she could sense. He was also an ambassador from Angus and she trusted her uncle to choose his allies wisely, even if this one didn't look able to withstand the weather. While he stood with rain dripping from his nose, she wondered how well he might stand up to a vicious opponent.

However, he was her only aid for the present and there was something in his face that she liked. 'It's Ian Og,' she explained. 'I can feel that something has happened to him. He's gone and I don't know where, but that soldier we are following knows about it.

There's something bad going on. They tried to kill poor Peter, you know!'

'Peter from the fort, the kitchen lad, you mean?'

'Yes, they beat him and were going to kill him.'

Having gained control of her feelings, Sarah told him more of the day's happenings as they moved quietly through the bushes and scrub parallel to the road. By the time they reached the next safe hiding place, Hamish realised his mission was likely to be much more complicated than Angus could have anticipated.

CHAPTER 5

THE PERSISTENT DRIZZLE HAD increased to a downpour by the time Lenny Dickens returned to the remains of the drover's camp. Scorched earth and wood ash was all that was left of last night's fire. Had MacCannie been dissatisfied he would have waited, and there would have been an immediate reckoning. He sat down and started drinking the whisky he had bought at the ale house in the town.

The soldier tried unsuccessfully to reassure himself that Peter hadn't survived his boat trip. If the pious lad had managed to return to the fort, there would be further charges to face. The Highland boy was alone when Ash caught him, and he hoped that pointed to Peter's demise.

As he left the shelter of the ruined castle, he saw an old woman crouched in her cowhide under the shade of a big oak. It was not yet in leaf, but the lower branches were broad and she was hunched facing the tree, so that only her back met the wind and rain.

He went over to her. 'Where did they go?' he shouted. 'Where did they go?' The drunken kick that accompanied his words was hardly vicious, but if it had connected fully, it would have caused severe distress to his victim.

Sarah and Hamish, who were in pursuit, took shelter behind some trees to watch. Involuntarily they winced when he kicked the old woman, but the sooty grey heap did not respond. The multitude of coverings may have provided some protection, but she would not give the bully the satisfaction of showing any fear.

Hamish told Sarah to stay where she was, and then sprinted towards the two, calling out, 'Granny! Granny! Is that you?' He rushed past the soldier and in Scots added as he knelt down, *'Thank you for finding her. We were so worried.'*

The fat man looked at him in astonishment, and fortunately did not see the matching look of incomprehension from his victim. *'If she's your granny, you keep her under control. She's a troublemaker. She was going to attack me.'* Looking down at the woman he continued, *'Weren't you? You old witch!'*

The smiling ginger-haired youth did not seem to be at all intimidated by Dickens. The man could have felled him with one arm, but something which glittered from within the lad's steady gaze held him back. At last the frustrated soldier lowered his raised fist, and, with a shake of his head, turned on his heel and made for the road.

It was with relief that Sarah saw Dickens leaving. She'd kept herself well hidden until he was safely out of sight. Hamish beckoned her to join them.

He bent down to the old woman and spoke gently. 'Hello Jeannie. It's Hamish and this is Sarah.'

'I don't know any Hamish. I don't know any Sarah.'

'You know me, Jeannie.' His tone was soothing. 'Many a time you showed me where to find the wild bee honey. You remember?'

Although the affronts of Private Dickens were not forgotten, she was willing to let her anger cool a little.

'Now, Red-haired Ruach, I hope you're not like that man. He has no manners at all.' She stood up, regally drew the cowhide more tightly around her, then leaned closer and whispered, 'Have you a wee bit of snuff on you, Ruach?'

When Hamish shook his head, she snorted with impatience but stopped when he said, 'I have some crowdie, if you would like it.' As he spoke he reached into his sporran and brought out a small leafy bundle, and peeled off a corner to show the crumbly white cheese within.

She took it and tucked it into the folds of her wrapping. Sarah was astonished to observe the marked change in the old woman, who now stood more erect as she said, 'Ah yes, Hamish Ruach MacNeil. Is your mother well?'

'Yes. She is keeping well. My sisters and I are looking after her.'

Jeannie turned to look at Sarah. She eyed her up and down and said, 'Are you married, Ruach? Is this your wife? She's bonnie. I hope you will have a happy life together.'

'No, she's not my wife. She is on her way to The Weaver's house at Achintore, and we have lost her brother. He seems to have disappeared.'

'Did you see him, Jeannie?' asked Sarah tearfully. 'My wee brother Ian Og?'

'Ah … so that's what it was.' Jeannie nodded as

realisation of what she had witnessed dawned on her. 'Yes … When the drovers were leaving, two of them headed towards Glen Nevis. The dark one, Hugh they called him, had a lumpy bundle over his shoulder. That would be your brother, I think.'

It took a few moments for Sarah to take in what had been said. In the meantime Jeannie began to lay out her hides and scraps of cloth. Within the folds she found a bannock. It looked as grey as herself. 'Here' she offered it to them. 'It is for your journey to Kinlochmore … Yes, Kinlochmore. That's where they're going. They wish ill on someone there.'

As they were trying to absorb the full meaning of her words, the two thanked her with smiles and refused the gift, which she started to nibble before throwing it back into one of her bundles. She sighed and seemed to be shrinking back into herself again as she gathered everything around her.

It was time to be on their way. 'Will you come with us, Jeannie?' Hamish asked.

She looked at him, turned on her heel and muttered, 'What about your sisters? Poor girls, poor girls, poor girls' as she hastened away towards the side of the castle where some drovers were camped.

Sarah asked many questions about old Jeannie. Hamish could only say that she was just as he remembered when he was growing up. 'She was always wandering the hills and glens around Lochaber. People would take her in, but she wouldn't stay for more than one night because she was always looking for her family.'

'What happened to them?' asked Sarah. As they walked, Hamish told her that Jeannie was born in Glencoe only five years before the massacre took place there in 1692. Although they were warned by one of the soldiers, and got out of the village before the slaughter took place, the family died of cold before they could get to shelter. Almost frozen, the only survivor, Jeannie was found curled up among the bodies, and never believed they were dead. Since then she was always looking for them.

'That's very sad,' Sarah said. 'I've heard about Jeannie but I never knew the full story.'

'Yes, it was a tragedy, and many families suffered,' said Hamish.

Sarah stopped walking. 'We have to find Ian Og. What will they do to him?' Her face fell. She had been so intent on looking for Ian Og that the original purpose of her journey had been lost. She had forgotten all about her auntie.

'Oh no, I was quite forgetting about Auntie Kate, and Angus will be mad. What am I to do? I have to find Ian Og before anything happens to him.' The words began to tumble out of her. 'God knows how he could end up if no one is there to save him. Angus would know what to do, but he's not here.'

As she panicked her voice rose. 'Auntie Kate will have others there to help her, but Ian Og has no one. I'll have to go after him.' She gathered her plaid more firmly around her, and began to run towards the open mouth of Glen Nevis. She was twenty yards away before she turned to Hamish and called out. 'You can go and tell Angus.'

These were not Angus's instructions to Hamish, and he knew that Angus would no longer be in the town. Nor would he be pleased if he thought that Hamish abandoned Sarah and let her walk the hills alone. 'Wait!' he called. 'Wait a minute.'

When he caught up with her, he pulled her arm. 'Will you listen?' She yanked her arm away and carried on walking, head down, so that he would not see the tears on her face, which were beginning to mingle with the steady rain.

'Sarah, stop!' This time he held on to her wrist and made her look at him. 'This is no way to go about things. We have to talk. The old woman may have got it wrong, and you could be wandering the hills for days on a wild goose chase.'

He hesitated, trying to think of other reasons why she should not be allowed to go off on her own. 'Besides which,' he added ruefully. 'Angus isn't in the town to tell. He had to go to Inverlochy and buy some grain. He took Pepper, and left your bundle at my house. We have to collect it, and get you down to your Auntie Kate. You're the one she needs. You can't disappear like Ian Og.'

There was no denying the truth of this. There came a lump in Sarah's throat as she tried to keep a hold on herself. Her instincts told her that Jeannie was right and Ian Og was in severe danger. Hamish was right too, and there was little choice but to make for the town, and then get to Auntie Kate's as duty called. She would have to put her trust in Hamish.

'I promised I'd get you there. And that is what I have to do.' said Hamish firmly. 'Then I'll go looking for Ian Og. I promise.'

'It'll be too late.' Sarah shook her head. 'By the time we get to Auntie Kate's in Achintore we'll have no way to guess which way they took him.' With a noisy sniffle she pressed forward, dripping wet from head to toe with her hair stuck in streaks to her forehead. Hamish was struck by how determined she looked, bravely facing the cruelty of life. His arm came up around her shoulder and he gave her a comforting squeeze.

Sarah hardly noticed. She'd been thinking and now she had a plan.

'I don't need you to take me to Auntie Kate's house.' Her eyes sparkled. 'Ian Og needs you more.' The idea was simple. 'You must go after him. I can fetch my bundle from your house. It won't take long, and I can tell your mother what's happened so that she won't be worrying. Then I can go on to Auntie Kate's. I only have to go down the side of the loch, and a couple of miles beyond the dyers' burn.'

As he listened to her words, Hamish could think of no valid reasons to oppose her suggestion. The fire of hope within her eyes would have overcome greater men. Angus would be cross, but he would understand there was no alternative. There was only one problem: Lizzie, his Mammy. She wouldn't worry about letting Sarah travel alone on strange roads, but she would be impossible if Hamish was not under her thumb. A pinched white face with a tight determined mouth floated into his mind's eye. Only slowly was it eroded by another image: Sarah's tear-stained face and hopeful look, in front of him. There was no question as to what he would do, and he would face the music when he returned.

A few minutes later, as the rain was easing, Sarah skirted the parade ground, and took the track up the hill on the edge of the settlement. She was thankful it wasn't far to Hamish's home. Like most of the houses in the town, it was built of stones, with mud and rush thatch. To Sarah's eyes, it was much neater than the stony sprawl that made up her own home in Glen Rowan.

Trying to remember Hamish's instructions, she knocked at the open half-door and blessed the house. Three girls crowded around the low door. The tallest assured her that it was indeed the home of Lizzie MacNeil. She was due home at any moment, if Sarah would like to come inside and shelter from the weather.

In the main room the damp day and wind conspired to ensure that blue peat smoke from the fire hung in the air. Margaret, the middle of the three children, dusted the stool beside the fire. When Sarah said that she had only come to collect her bundle which Uncle Angus Sticks left with them, the girls wanted to hear all about her adventure. They heard all the gossip about Alistair Glic in the town, and the boat in the harbour. Duncanina, the youngest, remembering her manners, brought Sarah a cup of ale, before going out on the track to see why Hamish was lagging.

While she slaked her thirst, Sarah told them that Hamish had gone to fetch Ian Og, who was on guard further up the river, and that he would be home as soon as he could. Under their questioning, she gave only the bare bones of rescuing young Peter and made no mention of climbing into the fort, only that Peter was helped to safety. This much the whole town was likely to know already.

The three girls wanted to know all about her journey and the family in Glen Rowan. As she chatted with them, Catriona, mistress of the house while her mother was out, offered Sarah some brose. She gratefully accepted the bowl of uncooked oatmeal, happy to note that it had been mixed with stock rather than water.

Despite their gracious welcome, Sarah felt her heart beat faster when she heard the sound of footsteps. She stood up and turned to smile as Hamish's mother entered. Lizzie MacNeil was a small woman with streaked grey hair tied back tightly with wooden pins. She would have been quite attractive had years of frowning not left many lines on her face. Her piercing look was that of a foraging rat, and despite the tight smile there was no warmth at all from her.

'You're Angus's niece.' It was a statement rather than a question and she added curtly, 'We could all see you cavorting in that boat.' Then looking around, she asked, 'Where's Hamish? Is he not here yet?'

Sarah felt that the woman could see into her soul. 'No. He went to fetch Ian Og.' The less she said, the less to be quizzed upon, or blamed for later, but Lizzie was not to be put off.

'Fetch him from where?'

Sarah kept as close to the truth as she dared. 'I'm not sure.' The vague reply was an attempt to hide how nervous she was. 'He was waiting for us along the river but we couldn't find him.'

'Why didn't you wait for them? You could all have come together.'

Sarah found the directness of the questions disconcerting and tried to keep her answers just as direct.

'We were getting worried about Auntie Kate. So Hamish felt it was better if I came on ahead. And he wanted you to know he was safe.' Sarah hoped this would be reassuring to the woman, but it didn't seem to satisfy her at all.

She asked sharply, 'What would he be doing that would not be safe? Why did you say that? Was there other foolishness?'

'Oh no, not at all.' Sarah tried to think. 'No foolishness.' This at least was true. 'Just that he was delayed and he did not know how long he would be, and he didn't want you to be concerned.'

Lizzie wasn't happy at all with this reply. As she frowned, Sarah could see all the lines on her face grow even sharper, converging on the pinched white nose.

'Well, I need him and he's not here. He's just like his father. God be good to him.'

As the blessing thoughtlessly tripped off her tongue, it sounded to Sarah's ears more like a curse.

'I'm sure he'll be here as soon as he can. Ian Og will be anxious to get back as quickly as possible as well.'

'Is he feckless, your Ian Og?'

Sarah thought it was an odd way to talk to her about her brother. 'Oh no, not at all,' she assured her. His smiling face came to mind and she felt the tears begin to well up. She rushed to get some words out to stop herself crying. 'He's very sensible. It was just unfortunate that when Alistair left, we weren't together.'

'Alistair Glic ... Ye-es. He is too tricky for his own good, that one, if you ask me,' Lizzie snorted, and although Sarah felt this was unfair, the change of subject was a relief. It was clear from her disapproving sniff that she did not have a high opinion of Alistair. Sarah excused herself by saying that her Auntie Kate would be worrying about her and took her leave. Young Duncanina cheerfully offered to take her down beyond the town by way of a shortcut she knew, and Sarah was pleased to accept. She had no wish to meet any more soldiers.

With her precious bundle tied across her back, she bade the family farewell, promising to call in to collect any messages on her way home. Soon the two girls were walking quickly westwards. The younger girl quite understood the need for speed. She kept up the blether about the family, Hamish and Alistair Glic until they reached the point where they stood looking down on the higgledy-piggledy mess of shelters and vats beside the dyers' stream. The shore track lay below.

'Safe journey to you,' said Duncanina formally, before impulsively throwing her arms around Sarah. 'I think you were very brave to stand up to the soldiers, and help Peter get back to the fort.'

This warm-hearted gesture took Sarah by surprise. She wanted to cry out that she was heartbroken with worry about Ian Og, but instead she held the girl tightly, before scrambling away down the side of the stream. She turned around with a wave for the kind Duncanina, before disappearing out of sight altogether.

CHAPTER 6

IT WAS EARLY EVENING when Sarah walked, exhausted, up the grassy slope to The Weaver's house. She was admiring the long stone building nestling under neat thatch, when a barefoot boy shot out from the far side of the building. Like a startled goose, he was running and waving his arms, scattering several hens in his path. His ragged plaid hardly covered him and flapped wildly in his wake. Zigzagging towards the astonished Sarah, splashing through puddles, he brandished a stick and yelled over and over the war cry of the Camerons: 'Children of the hounds come here and get flesh.' A tan lurcher, barking all the while, ran with him.

Sarah stood still. She had paid little attention when Uncle Angus often talked about wee Donuill Dhu. Eventually, she remembered the motto of the Camerons. 'Unite together,' she cried out. The boy stopped his charge immediately, and waited in silence looking up at her. The dog took a moment longer to slither to a halt, and then stood there wagging its tail.

The boy was daft, like Uncle Ranald. There was great difference in age, but in his eyes the same blank innocence. She smiled cautiously down at the two. Boy and dog matched her smile and continued to wait, effectively barring the way. When she made a move to pass, he frowned and stepped back a pace to block her, and then grinned again. The dog came beside him, tail still wagging. The stalemate seemed to last forever. Sarah wanted to scream at the boy, the dog, the whole world. Fortunately, Kate herself had spent the day waiting with increasing anxiety for sounds of the boy's welcome.

She came to the door as quickly as her pregnant girth allowed and threw it open, calling out through the damp air. 'Well done, Donuill Dhu!' With a great emphasis to Sarah, she added, 'Isn't he great at guarding us?'

'Oh yes, indeed,' agreed a relieved Sarah, who'd only heard Angus speak of the password, but not of the praise required. 'I never met a better guard.' The young lad, content that his duty was done, fell into step beside her, and matched strides for the last few muddy yards to the house.

The dog, realising its sport was over, scampered off around the far side of the building, ignoring the indignant hens. At the door the boy turned away and followed his companion, whistling tunelessly and tapping his stick on the wall of the house, beating time to an air only he could hear.

Until her marriage seven years ago, Dadda's sister Kate had been like a second mother to Sarah. Now heavily pregnant, she was no longer the willow wand Sarah remembered, but the warm smile was still that of her own Auntie Kate.

'But where's Angus and Ian Og?' asked Kate.

Sarah's words jumbled out to form an incoherent tale of the day's happenings. It took Kate several minutes to make any sense of it. With an arm around Sarah she drew her into the house and unharnessed the bundle. Removing the wet plaid she sat her beside the fire, before filling two bowls with whisky and setting one into her hands. 'Drink' she said. Obediently, Sarah sipped the fiery liquid. The red peat fire against the inner wall radiated a welcome nearly as warm as Donuill Dhu's, but Sarah's misery wrapped her in a chill shroud.

A marvellous aroma of chicken broth coming from the pot hanging on its chain above the embers of the fire infused the whole house. On the table there were oat and barley bannocks made fresh that day.

Kate gradually garnered more details of the day from Sarah. As she pondered the events she was able to point out that when old Jeannie saw Ian Og being carried off, he was alive. Had murder been the cattlemen's intention they could have done it at the river, and short of death, Ian Og would soon make his escape, with or without Hamish's help. The words barely comforted the distressed Sarah. Kate refilled the bowl with whisky, hoping it might ease her pain.

By the time the staid and stocky figure of Donald Cameron, known by all as The Weaver, finally shouted the password for Donuill Dhu, it was dark. By now Auntie Kate knew every last detail of the day's events. While they sat around the table, The Weaver eventually pieced together the story. He nodded or shook his head at the telling of each event. Sometimes the sound of his indrawn breath betrayed his concern, and several times he patted Sarah's hand. Normally taciturn, he waited until the two ran out of words before turning with a wry smile to Kate.

'I'll need food in me if I'm to go out again.' The women rose as one, each apologising for not seeing at once to his hunger. Sarah soon had thick meaty broth ladled into a bowl, and Kate laid a couple of the fresh oat bannocks beside him, and put another two into his sporran. Ale and whisky were also set on the table.

There was silence for a moment as the three bowed their heads. The Weaver blessed the food he was about to eat, thanked God for His bounty and requested the safe keeping of Ian Og and others during the coming night. As he picked up the spoon he nodded to Kate. 'I'll take "The Bull" with me. He's a good man on the hill.'

It was a signal. Kate filled two more big wooden bowls with broth. 'Come' she told the bemused Sarah. 'I could use a hand and we need a lanthorn.' Clutching one of the bowls she led the way in the dark to the byre outside.

It was considered a comfortable lodging by young Donuill Dhu and his uncle The Bull, whose wrinkled face looked like a tired apple, but his big gap-toothed smile for Kate was friendly, and he nimbly produced a stool for her. While Sarah handed her bowl to the young one, Kate passed hers to the elder and told him that his help would be needed in the search for Ian Og. He asked no questions, knowing that The Weaver would tell him all the details and consider his advice later.

In the house The Weaver was ready to leave. Had Kate not been so pregnant, he might have shared his misgivings about what he'd heard in the town. After Peter returned to the fort, one of the soldiers was put under guard, while the other, a thoroughly bad lot, was seen heading drunkenly up the new road towards

Kinlochmore. At other times The Weaver might have made light of a boy missing for the night. There were plenty of deer to chase and hares to hunt. A lively boy might easily lose track of time, but this was different.

Confidently, he predicted that the kidnappers could not get far, but the strange events of the day gave him a bad feeling which he was at pains to hide. As he was speaking, man and boy sidled into the room. The Weaver looked down first at the lad and instructed him that while his uncle was away he was in charge of the beasts. Donuill Dhu straightened himself importantly before withdrawing. Kate handed two bannocks to The Bull and without comment he too slipped outside to wait.

With a close embrace for his dear Kate and a more formal squeeze of the shoulder for his niece, 'Take care of her' was all The Weaver said as he turned and left the croft. It was too dark to start a search tonight, but in Maryburgh the pair could gather men and in the morning they would find Hamish and follow the kidnappers' trail.

Sarah's mind was eased to hear Uncle Donald giving solid and sensible explanations, but when the two figures disappeared into the darkness along the loch side, a great deal of her courage left with them.

Kate finally persuaded her to lie down in the curtained bed, which was in the corner of the big room, and after saying their night prayers together she, left. She hauled her aching, swollen body beyond the weaving room to the small bedroom at the end of the house.

Sarah was too sad to notice the graciousness of her surroundings. She lay on the bed, which was raised off the ground. It had a deep linen bag of straw for comfort and two warm woollen blankets to cover her. At home, piles of heather or bracken gathered on the earthen floor made warm-enough nests. Plaids were the main covering, and at night each child curled up in a favourite place, and they were not shy to snuggle up to visitors if warmth were needed.

It was lonely in the fine bed, so Sarah drew the curtain aside and watched the red tinges fading within the remains of the fire, and tried to compose herself for sleep. There was tension in her gut. Only the comforting feel of warm rosary beads stopped her from keening with grief. Fingers automatically turned each round wooden piece as she asked God to protect young Ian Og. Eventually her despair gave way to restless dreams.

CHAPTER 7

Hamish settled into a measured run towards Glen Nevis when Sarah left. His gangly legs quickly covered ground. From time to time he stole a look behind him. It wasn't long before Sarah was lost to his view, but sparkling greenish-hazel eyes lined with black lashes stayed in his mind.

The ground was muddy under his brogues, but it didn't slow him down. Soon he was running along the floor of the glen beside the fickle Nevis River. Sometimes it flowed slowly between wide banks. At other parts it narrowed and developed speed to cascade over mighty rocks. There was a crossing near a big house. He waved a greeting to the woman sitting at a window as he passed.

Old Aggie Cameron had sat at that window all through his boyhood. As a youngster he feared her, and made a sign against the evil eye whenever he passed that way. Now, he knew her knees and ankles were so swollen and sore, that each day her sons lifted her to sit at the window so that she might be diverted by whatever she could see happening all around the glen. However, Hamish still made a sign against the evil eye, because he feared that the curse which was upon her might still come upon him.

Further along the way he met Blind John, one of her sons, and asked what travellers, if any, he had seen passing up on the track towards the great waterfall. John wasn't actually blind. The nickname was earned many years ago when he questioned the skill of a shinty goalkeeper, saying, 'Even if I was blind, I could have defended that goal better.' Since then he had been known as Blind John. Ironically, Hughie Cameron, his cousin, who was in goals that day, was thereafter known as The Goalie.

Blind John told Hamish that he had seen some drovers, who said they were heading for the falls at the head of the glen, but later he'd seen some of them going up the hill towards the Fairy Fort. Hamish thanked him and, deep in thought, continued trotting along the track. If the drovers were split, there was no way of guessing which group had Ian Og. Jeannie said they were going towards Glen Nevis, which would favour the track beside the falls at the head of the glen, but she also said there was to be mischief, and this might cause a man to lie about his route, and cut over another hill instead.

Pursuit would be difficult. Cattle trails crossed in every direction. There was a path that divided at the hill of Creag Bhreac: the eastern trail joined others in Glencoe while the western one led down to North Ballachulish at the narrow entrance to Loch Leven. A fugitive might take himself south towards Onich, west to the narrows at Corran, or even back towards Maryburgh and the fort.

When Hamish reached the fork in the track, he was determined to take the shorter route towards the inn on Rannoch moor. If there was to be a meeting, he would be among the first to get there. As he turned eastwards, some hooded crows caught his eye: five of them, feeding together on an old fox carcass, taking turns to scramble up and peck pieces from it. As he approached, they rose together and moved ahead of him. When his steps brought him closer they didn't fly back to the carrion, instead they all circled forward again and landed several yards further on. They kept up this behaviour right to the fork in the track. Together they rose and flew towards the graveyard before alighting onto trees and bushes, where they stayed almost motionless. There they waited, dark-capped heads all pointed towards him.

Although he pressed ahead on the main path for a few steps, Hamish could feel the crows staring at him. He held traditional beliefs and so whatever signal the crows were trying to give him, good or ill, he was fated to follow their lead. Their presence meant danger, and he would have to be on his guard, but he could not ignore such a clear sign. Reluctantly he turned towards the side track. The crows didn't move. They watched him until he reached the trees and began to climb up through the fallen rocks and old bracken. Together they rose cawing into the air, and then flew off back in the direction of the carcass they were feeding on earlier. Hamish resolved to keep this story of the crows to himself. It was strange and he knew people would not believe him.

The track up the hill was steep and not often used. His leg muscles were tiring as he steadily picked his way, following the edge of a small stream. Although the rain had stopped, he needed to take care on the stones because they were slippery. Behind him on the other side of the glen, the upper slopes of Ben Nevis, grey and rocky, occasionally emerged from behind the clouds.

It looked as if an army could have climbed on this rough stony trail without leaving any evidence, and as Hamish clambered upwards, he was concerned that his faith in the crows might have been misplaced. After an hour's climbing he could still see no hint of any other travellers, and his dejection grew. It wasn't until he passed the jumble of ancient stones they called the Fairy Fort when at last there was a fresh print. Rain had softened some ground and there was the clear impression of a square heel. No highlander's cuaran or brogue would be so sharply embedded. It was the boot print of a soldier. There were no other signs of recent passage, and nothing to show that Ian Og had been brought this way, but Hamish felt relieved. At least he wasn't chasing shadows.

Remembering there would be a price to pay at home for this escapade made his cheerful mood dissipate. Since his father died, his mother leant more and more upon him, spurning the advice of other members of the family. She would be tormented by his absence, and his punishment would be to have her tell him again and again how frightened she was, not for herself, but for him. The thought of such crippling concern being rehashed in the weeks ahead would have caused him to abandon his mad quest, but with the image of a tear-stained Sarah, he gritted his teeth and kept going.

Hamish was thankful when he reached the top of the steep track. Here the slope of the land was less treacherous and he could cover more distance before darkness fell. The cattle track was not far from the Fairy Fort. All was green from the new spring growth and damp from the rain. In the coming weeks, herds would spread on either side of the main track, and leisurely graze their way to Rannoch and the south.

He took a deep breath and began a steady run, which took him across soft grass, through wet bogs and alongside treacherous crags. Only when it was becoming dark did he stop by a rocky stream, take a drink and think about settling himself down for the night.

He heard a sound and a fat, familiar frame appeared from behind a rock.

'Well, well, what have we got here?' It was ill fate which led Lenny Dickens to shelter at the same mountain stream.

After leaving Jeannie and the lad claiming to be her grandson close to the drover's camp, Lenny Dickens took careful thought about his future in General Handasyd's regiment. On the way back to the fort, he realised grimly that Colonel Campbell wouldn't need Peter's testimony to convict him of stealing from the stores. There were others with serious grudges against him who would relish the prospect of seeing him receive a flogging, and if all his misdemeanours came to light, he might even be hanged.

Often he'd mulled over the fact that Fort William was a lonely place, with little scope for an entrepreneur like himself. The few women allowed to follow the soldiers showed little interest in his direction. The local ones were too wild for him to take a chance with, although there were one or two young girls around the town, who looked, in his opinion, as if they needed a real man to take them in hand. He'd tried his luck with one young girl, but her screams were heard by more squeamish soldiers who pulled him away from her, and brought him back, protesting, to the barracks. He'd worn the scratches for a couple of weeks and was given a wide berth by all the town's women after that. It was said that sober he was mean and violent, and when drunk he was even worse. It was a reputation he defended proudly, but one which had landed him in trouble with the colonel more than once.

Back in the fort he retrieved his stash of coins from behind a brick in the stable wall, then made one last trip to the store, stealing enough tobacco and food to last him a month, and a cape to protect himself from the worst of the weather, which made him look even more rotund. He brazenly walked back out the gates of the fort with his musket slung over one shoulder. 'I won't be long,' he called to the sentry and left without a further glance behind him.

At the alehouse he bought two flasks of the whisky which Angus had delivered that morning, and he set out on the long march towards Kinlochmore, where he was to meet again with MacCannie. When he stopped to rest at the mountain stream near Blarmafoldach, the first flask of whisky was already inside him, and the injustices of the day were beginning to mount up in his imagination.

The gangly youth's red hair seemed familiar. Even in the half-darkness he could see the look of determination on the face. The sight of this bright-eyed, brass-necked lad, who had boldly stood between him and the old woman, was the final straw.

'*A dirty little rebel, I'd say,*' he sneered and before Hamish realised what was happening, a musket butt crashed onto his shoulder. Caught off balance, he fell sprawling to the ground. A hefty boot swung towards his ribs. Hamish rolled over to avoid it, but took the blow on his side. He swallowed hard to stop the vomit rising. He tried to scramble away, but he couldn't make his limbs act quickly enough. His belt snapped and his plaid got tangled around him.

'Not so cocky now, eh?' Dickens mocked. He had the youth at his mercy, and stepped on the loose fabric to hold his prey. He brought back his foot to deliver another vicious kick and for a moment Hamish hesitated, in thrall. Fortunately, his instinct urged him to a great effort and he rolled again away from his attacker towards the steeper edge of the track and then over the side, dragging his clothing with him.

It was the bully's turn to be off balance. Drunkenly he fell with a thud onto the loose end of the plaid and was carried over the edge. Youth, man and plaid rolled down the rocky scree. At the bottom where the slope met level ground, Hamish came to a halt. He was winded and, apart from his brogues, naked. He felt as if he'd been skinned alive. The pain from the kicking was spreading over his whole body, and he gasped desperately to try and catch his breath.

A moment later, Dickens came to rest several feet away. He was unhurt, but the fall only provoked his temper further. *'You little bastard,'* he growled, and then when he saw that Hamish wasn't moving, rose to his feet and smiled in anticipation. *'I have you now, boy, I'd say.'* Then with sarcasm he added. *'You and your granny.'*

The soldier wasn't a tall man, but from where Hamish lay sprawled, he was a giant. There was no getting away now. He tried to scramble backwards using his feet, but his breathing was only just beginning to come right again, and his damaged ankle wouldn't respond.

Grinning, Dickens towered over him and was set for the kill, but he wasn't prepared for the determined kick Hamish landed on his knee with his good leg. It was a mighty blow, and down the man went, landing with a wallop on his backside, sprawled beside the exhausted youth. His dignity rather than his person was injured, and now there was murder in his eye. He reached over with one great ham fist and grasped Hamish's neck. *'You're a dead rebel now, I'd say.'*

The words were spoken with slow resolve into the face of his victim. Hamish could smell the stale stench of whisky as each word was rasped out. Then those sneering lips abruptly went slack when Hamish smashed a rock squarely into the side of his head.

Without taking his eyes off the face in front of him, Hamish hit him again as hard as he possibly could, drawing on all the resources of strength his desperation afforded him. Finally, Dickens slumped back heavily onto the stones, a bubbling moan in his throat.

Hamish closed his eyes tightly, and drew as deep a breath as his injured rib would allow. The dreadful gurgling groan coming from his enemy continued, and grew louder. Only one course of action lay open to him and he would have to act speedily if he wasn't to lose his nerve.

With an effort of will he opened his eyes and looked at the bloody rock still resting in his hand. He laid it down. There was a bigger, heavier rock nearby and he made himself stand up, ankle and rib throbbing, and fetched it. Normally, he would have had no difficulty carrying such a boulder, but it needed every effort of his will to pick it up. He gritted his teeth and struggled to bring it the couple of yards back to his foe, then dropped it. There was a dull hollow sound that resounded across the moor. The groaning stopped and the stone, its work done, rolled over to rest beside a bloody ear. Hamish swallowed again and again, as he tried to stop his stomach betraying him.

The deed must look like an accident, or there would be serious repercussions for the local clansmen and women. He took pebbles from beneath the boulder, to settle it more securely and arranged all the rest to look undisturbed. He removed his first rock, which clearly showed bloody handprints, and any other traces of a struggle. For the plan to work, others must think that, while he was drunk, Dickens lost his footing and hit his head when he fell.

Naked and bruised, Hamish limped across to the river which, through time, had carved itself a path in the side of the hill. Slowly, he stepped into the water and rinsed himself and the stone free of dirt and blood.

The icy water numbed his pain a little, and he threw the stone outward beyond the river as far as he could, and heard it rattle as it bounced over the rocks. His ankle wouldn't hold him much longer, but he returned to inspect the motionless Dickens.

'You were wrong, I'd say,' Hamish whispered in Scots. *'And I'm sure you wouldn't mind if I took some of your food, I'd say.'*

He then began to crawl painfully back up the slope, all the while thinking of Ian Og and how worried Sarah must be back at her auntie's house. As the last of the daylight faded from the sky, he retrieved his plaid from where it was caught on a rock. He draped it over one shoulder and then under the opposite arm. It was fortunate that there had been no other travellers passing. It looked as if Dickens had been alone, but Hamish could take no chances. If the soldiers caught him before he was safely hidden, there would be no mercy.

Many stories circulated about what happened to convicted rebels. Being shot or hanged would be the best he could hope for! Men like Dickens were known to play nasty games with prisoners. A blind eye was often turned when a rebel was held in the fort, and for lesser crimes than the deed he had just committed.

At the fort, Dickens's absence had been noticed. He'd been seen at the alehouse and later going up the hilly track towards Loch Leven. The general opinion was that with charges to face he was probably drowning his sorrows somewhere, and would creep in with a hangover the next morning.

Gradually Hamish reached the track above. He prayed that he was close to where his sporran and belt lay and tried to think straight. There was a sound among the trees on a hill near him. He froze. It came again and then there was the bark of a fox. He made himself take a breath and then another. His chest ached with the movement, and his heart thumped loud enough to drown out the other sounds of the night. He wondered if Dickens's soul was possessing the fox to give him a fright, but he would not let that man, dead or alive, frighten him enough to forget his task.

He crawled along, feeling for his missing items in the wet clumps of grass. Eventually, he touched the end of his belt which had his sporran still attached. The moon was gently shedding its light on the ground around him. Now he must shelter from hostile weather, hostile animals and hostile men.

Earlier he'd seen another outcrop of rock twenty or thirty feet above him. If he could get up there he would have a good view of the track but remain unseen. Despite the pain, his plan heartened him and he inched himself upwards, praying there would be no malevolent spirits. The spirit of Dickens was not the only one likely to roam these hills and glens.

Once at the top Hamish stopped. He thrust his swollen foot, still encased in its brogue, into a trickle of icy water flowing down between the rocks. The coldness took all feeling from his lower leg and he was able to attend to his injuries. Pulling out his broken belt and slowly unwinding his plaid, he let it fall beside him. Rummaging in his sporran, at the bottom he found what he was looking for, a small knife neatly sheathed in bark.

He used the knife to cut two strips from the plaid, one broad, the other narrow. Slowly he wrapped the first around his chest, groaning as he pulled it tight, and tucked in the free end as securely as he could. He felt dizzy and his chest felt as if a large hammer was striking at it. The bandage gave him some support, and he kept telling himself that soon he would be as good as new.

His ankle was black and blue and had swollen. Now, there was no question of removing his brogue. Carefully crooking his knee and bringing his shin back under his good leg, he could reach the foot without crushing his ribs more than necessary. Even so it was painful work, winding the makeshift bandage around leather, foot and ankle. Lethargy sapped both his strength and his will. It was a struggle, but at last the job was done.

His mouth was dry as dust, so very cautiously he changed his position to reach the water. With a cupped hand he scooped some to his parched lips. A sharp wind was blowing across the land, and he prayed that it was only the wind he could hear howling. He gave no thought to whether the sluggishness starting to overwhelm him, was tiredness or the effect of his injuries; he just knew that he must give in to it.

Hamish spent a long and fitful night. Although the vulpine soul of Dickens did not return to haunt him, there were moans from hanged clansmen, galloping headless horsemen, and a fairy piper playing the soulful lament 'Keppoch has lost his Bonnet.' Every time these ghastly noises awoke him, Hamish said his prayers and commended his spirit to God. He was greatly relieved when the first grey shafts of dawn banished the devils like Gabriel's mighty sword.

He sat up very slowly but immediately felt a burst of pain. It took a few moments for him to remember where he was and how he got there. He was hungry so he delved into his sporran to retrieve some of the food he had taken from Dickens. Sure that he was on the right track now, Hamish sighed: the kidnappers were much further ahead.

CHAPTER 8

GOLIATH'S PUFFING AND grunting told Ian Og when the party left flat ground, and was making its way up any hilly tracks. Sometimes they moved through bushes where he was carelessly scratched by passing branches. There was little breath wasted on conversation until they were moving on flat ground again. Even then, the men didn't talk much, keeping their energies for the journey. Ian Og felt a black pit opening within his head, into which he was likely to sink without trace. Staying hopeful and alert was difficult.

The men appeared intent on reaching their destination before nightfall and when they stopped again to rest, he was unceremoniously dumped on stony ground. He had no idea what they were doing, but he was thirsty and his bladder needed relief. He tried to yell in protest. Hardly a moan came out, but it was enough to attract the attention of his captors.

'*He's making a noise!*'

'*Finish him off now.*' It was the impatient voice of Goliath. '*I don't see why we have to bring him alive.*'

MacCannie was quite definite. *'No. We need lots of blood. It'll have to be there.'*

'We could get an animal.' It was the forlorn argument of one who knows he has lost

'Oh yes. There'll be one just standing there when we need it.' There was more than a hint of irony. *'No ... the boy alive is what we need.'*

The conversation was casual and Ian Og understood most of what was being said. An icy wave engulfed him as he listened to the men calmly discussing his death. Goliath, with a sigh, hoisted the terrified boy up and then swore, and roughly dropped him back down.

'Oh no, now he's pissed himself. I hope he didn't shit himself as well. I'm not carrying him if he's done that.' There was the sound of sniffing and eventually agreement that Ian Og had not done worse than urinate.

'Well, Ken. I think it's your turn to carry him now anyway.' Goliath grinned.

'Oh no, it's not!' The younger one was quick to protest. *'I've got the pistols and the rest. I'm minding the dogs as well.'*

'Well, I'll carry those things, and you can take a turn to carry the boy.'

As they squabbled, Ian Og just wanted this terrible nightmare to end, and wished he had not been so easily betrayed by his body. Distraught, he began to cry. The tears gushed from him as if to rival his urine. But suddenly, he sensed a strange presence. Abruptly his tears stopped as he could hear familiar words: 'Come on boy. You're not going to just lie there, are you? There's work to be done.'

They were the words of Granny Morag. He stopped himself from crying out. She couldn't possibly be there with him, but the words were definitely hers.

She used them in the morning, every morning. He'd often moaned to himself that she always used the same words every day.

'You're not going to just lie there, are you? There's work to be done.' The words rang in his ears. He felt the same weary resignation that came to him every day. There was work to be done and he must start to do it. His plaid was wet from the rain, but while the men were arguing, he could keep working on the belt at his wrists.

With a glimmer of new hope, he felt that the belt on his wrists was becoming a little slacker. Again, he felt Granny Morag's presence. 'That's more like it.' As he concentrated on his wrists, he realised that somehow it was just possible to see out beyond the plaid. The cloth had become like a blur over his glazed eyes, and he could see an impression of what was beyond. He knew it was miraculous.

'Thank you, Granny,' he murmured.

Despite this ghostly intervention, there was no magical release of his wrists. It was only a few minutes before MacCannie intervened between the other two, and the journey on Goliath Hugh's shoulder began again.

It was hard to keep vigilant, and Ian Og really didn't want to hear what they were planning to do with him so he concentrated on freeing his wrists, pulling and twisting, ignoring the pain, pulling again.

'*Alistair Glic. You hate him.*' Ken, the nephew, said to his uncle.

'*Maybe,*' was MacCannie's non-committal reply.

'*No, you do hate him,*' Ken insisted. '*Who'd go to such trouble? Me? I'd just kill him. Slit his throat one day when he wasn't looking.*'

'*You! You'd never get near enough,*' MacCannie dismissed Ken's boast.

It was the last word for a while, but Ian Og knew now that all this was something to do with his cousin Alistair.

As the men pressed onward in silence, Ian Og's arms felt as if they were being pulled out of their sockets. He was cold and could no longer feel his feet, although there was warmth where his body pressed against the massive shoulder of Goliath, and he tried to will it into his limbs. His head was protected by the plaid, but all the movement was disorienting him and the strange miracle of seeing through the cloth didn't happen again.

The men were paying him no more attention than any other burden that had to be hauled over the hills. They neither fed nor watered him.

'*So Alistair Glic ran off the herd you stole?*' It was partly a question.

'*No, he didn't.*' MacCannie wasn't one for talking, but he had pride. '*He got the whole MacDonell of Keppoch clan to help him.*'

'*So why are you out to get him?*' It seemed a fair question.

'*If we get him, we'll be getting the pride of the clan,*' MacCannie snapped crossly, adding '*and I don't like his cocky face. I'm going to take pleasure in bringing him down.*' Normally this would have been enough to finish the conversation, but the younger man was persistent.

'*So who's this Frenchman?*'

'*No one you need concern yourself with.*'

The questioner was not put off. '*Is he a spy?*'

'*Yes ... No.*' There was obviously no simple answer. '*He's been working for the government for years.*'

'*The French government?*' Ken was eager to keep the conversation going. It shortened the miles.

'*No,*' MacCannie snapped at the man's ignorance. '*His Majesty's Government, but the Highland rebels don't know that, and they trust him with messages to the French government.*'

'*And he takes them to the King?*'

Wearily MacCannie replied, '*No. He takes them over to France, but he also passes anything of interest on to a man in Edinburgh.*'

'*And they don't know anything about it?*'

'*No. And that's enough questions.*'

Ken wouldn't take the hint. '*So how do you know there's a meeting?*'

'*Look. I said. You ask too many questions. If you weren't my nephew you'd be getting your throat cut right now. Let's just say I know that there has been news coming in from Inverness about some of the pro-government clans considering turning over to the other side.*'

There was a hint of suspicion in Ken's next question. '*Did you know about that when we were up in Inverness?*'

'*Maybe, I did. Now let it rest.*'

'*Wait a minute.*' Light was dawning on the young man. '*That's why we were in Inverness. I knew you set this up and all because that Alistair Glic took your herd.*'

This stung MacCannie into an angry outburst. '*That herd was worth a lot of money to me … to us, and he's going to be sorry. He'll be caught red-handed this time.*'

'*You can't be sure of that.*'

'*Oh yes I can.*' MacCannie's voice held barely re-strained rage. '*And if you don't shut your bloody mouth right now, I'll shut it for you, even if you are my nephew.*'

Ian Og was stunned. He was to be killed to take revenge against Alistair Glic, who thought he was to meet The Frenchman, but was really walking into a trap.

The idea that his cousin would come to harm kindled a new rage in the eleven-year-old boy. In that moment he became an adult. It no longer mattered to him whether he lived or died, but he resolved to make sure these men would never succeed.

Goliath Hugh finally threw his bundle down again, with a great sigh of relief. Ian Og thanked his Maker that the ground upon which he landed was grassy. He could hear the dogs sniffing their new surroundings.

'*Let's get a fire going.*' Ken sounded cheerful.

MacCannie replied, '*Have you learned nothing, boy?*'

Even though his wrists were burning with his efforts to get free, Ian Og managed a wry smile at the ignorance of MacCannie's nephew. A fire now would give away their position, not only to Alistair Glic, but to every man, woman and child in the area. Anything strange would be noted.

Ian Og had another reason for trying to smile. At long last he could feel real slackness at his wrists, and one of his hands had room enough to be withdrawn. They were no longer taking much notice of him. He concentrated hard to try and look out beyond the fabric of the plaid once more. The miracle didn't happen at first, and he tried to recall exactly how it might have been achieved the last time. It still wouldn't come at his command, and only when he was beginning to give up in exasperation did a faint vision of beyond begin to appear again. He was able to make out the three men several yards away, two dogs marking the trees around them, and the distant reflection of grey water.

His wrists were hidden from them all and slowly, painfully, he dragged his hands free of the vile binding.

He could have shouted with joy, but he was determined not to let these men get any hint of his efforts. It took a long time before his stiff ankles were within reach of his numb hands, made clumsy from being bound so long, but sheer willpower helped him to ignore the pain in his shoulders and wrists. It might be his only chance, and his life – and Alistair's – depended upon it.

The task was difficult, the knot was firm and his progress was very slow, but at last he could feel a loosening around his ankles and with it a sharp cramp. Had there still not been a gag around his mouth, his cry would have alerted the other three. He wanted to straighten his legs to ease the pain, but this would have drawn their attention, so with tears in his eyes he forced himself to stay immobile. The knot was not completely untied and he knew he would have to make sure that he was free of the rope before launching into any escape bid.

His captors settled down for the night. '*Soon, I'll take vengeance on Alistair Glic.*' MacCannie grinned as he spoke, adding, '*Let's drink to it.*'

They drank to it many times and eventually lapsed into a drunken slumber. While they slept, Ian Og continued to struggle with the rope and after a while he felt it was loose enough that if opportunity arose, he might be able to crawl for cover.

He was surprised the next morning when MacCannie and Goliath Hugh decided to go and check the meeting place. Ken, the hopeless nephew, was left on guard with the dogs. With the others gone, Ian Og knew that even if he managed to evade MacCannie's nephew, the lurchers would soon track him. Getting to water was his best chance, and cunning his only armour. The loch was too far so he prayed there would be some decent-sized streams close by. Escape would require at least a small depth of water, and a great deal of luck.

Ken moved to the edge of the clearing looking out in the direction the others had gone. Their absence made him uneasy, and nervously he kept looking into the surrounding trees. Each time he turned away Ian Og prepared to move, but each time, the nephew returned. Then at last he went further along the trail with the dogs, only occasionally looking back.

Through the fabric of the plaid, Ian Og watched the blurred image move out of sight with disbelief. Like an old man he rose carefully onto his two lifeless feet. Arms still bound around his chest by belt and plaid, he hobbled blindly into the trees. Painful wriggling got first one, and then the other arm free. He prayed the dogs would not return too soon.

He was now able to unbind the belt and finally the stinking plaid. No time to rejoice. Bundling cloth and belt together he limped along awkwardly, trying to ignore skinned wrists and bleeding ankles. As he pushed his painful way through the newly green willows, his ears were cocked for a cry of discovery.

The silence was broken by a shout of protest. When the three men returned together to the clearing, MacCannie immediately saw his absence. '*You fool,*' he roared, and then turned and felled his nephew with a mighty punch. Blood coursing from his broken nose, the younger man was left sprawled on the ground, and the kick that followed bore rage and frustration. Those who knew MacCannie in a state of anger would have said Ken was fortunate in having only two broken ribs. Had Goliath Hugh not intervened to separate them, and point out that the boy couldn't be far away, the younger man would not have got off so lightly.

The fugitive was already spurring himself into a run, onwards through trees and bushes, ignoring scratches and bruises. Mercifully, the stream he hoped for wasn't far. His lungs were nearly bursting by the time he reached it. It was shallow at that point, but further downstream it was deeper, where a lad could hide among the boulders in the water. Without pausing, Ian Og splashed in and headed for the deeper water.

Two bounding dogs reached the stream and waited, eagerly sniffing the ground. A very angry MacCannie came close behind with Goliath Hugh. The injured nephew limped in the rear, not daring to affront his uncle any further. The dogs snuffled up and down the edge of the water and turned questioningly towards MacCannie. Given the nod, they began to pick their way downstream, sometimes giving a yelp which brought the first two men to inspect their findings.

'*Steady now, steady,*' urged MacCannie. '*He's here somewhere and I want him.*' Unwillingly, his injured nephew followed the other two, all wading towards deeper water, making it cloudier as they plodded along.

Ian Og let go of his plaid which floated downstream, releasing its tell-tale scent to further confuse the dogs. Lying submerged in the dark water between some large boulders, he held his breath, when the others passed within a few feet of him. He made no movement in case it attracted the attention of eyes sharpened with evil intent. Once they were out of sight, he slowly untied his gag and straightened the length of cloth before winding the ends familiarly around his fingers. Forming it into a sling meant he was no longer entirely defenceless.

From the stream bed beneath him he selected several stones. Each one would count dearly. He often went hunting tasty small animals for the pot, and seldom missed his target. The cold rage within him intended to do more than just survive. He would warn Alistair and take revenge. Cold in body and emotion, he gritted his teeth and waited, hidden in the mountain stream, while men and dogs continued their search further downhill towards the loch.

As the sounds of the searchers grew faint, Ian Og knew he must leave the water and find a safe haven. He crawled out and took cover in a clump of wee trees. With stones in one hand and sling in the other, he was as prepared as he could ever be.

There was a crackle of breaking twigs. Someone was approaching. It was the injured nephew, who hadn't been able to keep up with the others. Ken had seen a slight movement on the hill and retraced his steps not daring to believe his good luck. Creeping up to catch his quarry and before he had the sense to raise the alarm, a missile struck his forehead with all the force that fear and anger brought to Ian Og's tired muscles. The nephew was felled unconscious, but he would live to bear the further scorn of MacCannie.

Ian Og didn't wait to see the result of his work. Alive or dead, when the dogs found the nephew they would be able to track the scent of the lad who toppled him. There was no sound yet from the others. Desperation inspired his thoughts. Trusting the lurchers would follow, he gathered up a good handful of deer droppings and smeared them all over his naked body. Carefully, he climbed up the slope and away from the loch. Descending on the other side, he found plenty more droppings and he trusted that the lurchers would not be the only ones confused.

Only willpower kept him going. No more words came through the ether from Granny Morag. The anger in his heart drove him forwards and he kept going for as long as he was able. He took rests when he found shelter in the bushes or trees, constantly checking to see if his pursuers were gaining ground on him. There was no sign of them but he still kept moving.

From time to time, he supped water from streams along his path. As the day began to turn to night, he saw a faint twinkle of light ahead. It had been a long two days with nothing to eat, and he had never felt so hungry. Exhausted, he decided to settle down and shelter among the bushes, until he learned whether he was among friend or foe.

CHAPTER 9

HAMISH ATE THE FOOD he had taken from Dickens, and looked down from his position high on the rocks. Below him, bushes, trees and streams gradually emerged from the waning darkness, until eventually the countryside was revealed again in all its splendour. The rocky slope he lay upon fell gradually to the grassy track, and then more steeply to a river hidden by trees, before it rose again near Loch Linnhe, which he knew lay beyond. To the west the trail rose and disappeared again over the tops of distant hills. The views were spectacular, but Hamish faced more immediate concerns.

With his belt broken it wasn't possible to wear his plaid properly, but by folding it in half like the filibegs of the local ironworkers, he was able to wind it around his hips and over one shoulder and under the opposite arm. The thought that Roman senators must have worn their purple togas like this brought a brief smile.

With an attempt to summon his resolve, he lodged the broken belt and sporran within the folds across his chest, and took a deep breath. Getting up was a struggle, and he had to support himself against the surrounding rocks before he could stand. He tried to put some of his weight onto his injured foot, but after a tentative step he fell back against the boulders, a spiral of pain shooting up his leg and overwhelming him.

Tears of frustration welled up in his eyes. There was little point in wishing he'd brought a stick. He would be as well wishing for the moon. If necessary, he would have to crawl his way down to the Blarmafoldach track. Folk there would ensure he got home safely. It was while he was trying to decide the best route for crawling through the heather that he spotted a sapling below, near some trees on the hillside. It looked perfect.

He shuffled down the slope, using his bad foot as little as possible to avoid extra pressure on his aching ribs, while trying to keep watch and remain alert. By the time he reached the ash plant, he was exhausted.

He concentrated on cutting out a strong stick to lean on. The knife in his sporran was very small and though it cut through the outer bark quite well, the inner meat of the little tree was tough. He kept shaving small pieces from it, and hoped that eventually he would be able to break it.

The work was slow, and as he finished he spied some soldiers coming up the track, carrying picks and shovels. In the town there was talk about another military road coming up over the hills here. These were probably a gang of workers sent to survey the land. He swore quietly, using words his mother would not have expected him to know. The men still had a long slope to face before he was in danger of being spotted, but in such a weakened condition, he would only have enough time to crawl painfully back up to his night-time hiding place.

Before he could move he heard a faint sound coming from the opposite direction. It was a distant *tumth … tumth … tumth …* of hooves. Hamish shuffled himself into the cover of the nearest heather. After a few nervous minutes, he saw a trim little garron trot into view, dwarfed by its rider. With relief coursing over him, he crawled as quickly as his damaged body would allow into Pepper's path.

For the pony, carefully picking her hooves between the stones, Angus's bulk was no more trouble than a pack of untaxed whisky. She was used to heavy loads and once on the road she would willingly trot all day.

Angus was pondering his grievances. He was still engrossed in maligning his young foster nephew, Alistair Glic, who disappeared with Sarah and Ian Og out on Loch Linnhe. At least Hamish could be trusted to find the young ones and deliver them safely to their Auntie Kate at Achintore. He had spent the night with cousin John Joe, who welcomed his company and happily provided shelter for his grain. Now he was heading for Mairin MacDonell, a distant cousin. For her, Angus was working harder than ever he had done in his life, distilling whisky and selling baskets, to gather enough money to propose marriage.

Only when the pony, without reference to him, changed pace and drew to a halt did he pay heed. It took a moment or two before he realised there was someone lying on the track, and another before he noticed the red hair and realised it was Hamish.

'Hamish! Hamish! What are you doing here?' Angus was puzzled. He looked around as he swung his leg over the bulky pack saddle to dismount. 'You gave me quite a turn.'

He put his arm forward to give the lad a hand to get up, and then realised he was injured. 'My God, boy, what happened?' He crouched to look more closely.

'Hush! There are soldiers beyond the bend,' said Hamish.

'Soldiers, did they do this? The dirty scoundrels,' Angus's voice swelled with injustice.

'It was a scoundrel alright, but he's a dead scoundrel now.' Speaking coherently was becoming an effort. 'He's down there.' Hamish nodded his head towards the slope where Dickens lay sprawled in the scrub.

Angus went to the edge of the track. 'Oh Lord save us! Are they looking for him? We'd better hide him.'

'No, no.' Hamish called out. 'There's no time. I made it look as though he fell. Get us out of here before they come.'

'Lean on me boy ... That's it.' Strong as an ox but gentle as a kitten, Angus helped Hamish onto his good foot, noting the white face and wince as Hamish gritted his teeth with the pain.

'We'll not get too far with you like that,' said Angus, bringing his whisky flask from his sporran, and taking a good thoughtful pull at it. His gaze travelled up and down the trail and he took another large gulp of the whisky, smacking his lips decisively. 'We'd never get away quick enough,' he said, handing the flask to Hamish. 'Get that into you,' he said and before Hamish could protest, added 'All of it, mind. I have an idea.'

When the soldiers came over the hill, they saw the stationary horse and two men waving enthusiastically. As they neared, it was obvious the older one was preventing the younger one from falling off the pack saddle, and the two of them were looking at something of great interest on the slope below them.

'*Good, you here now,*' said Angus in broken Scots as the men reached him, the words slurring slightly. '*He want look. He very drunk. I to get him home. His mother will kill me.*'

The soldiers knew Hamish from the town and had often seen Angus passing through, so the two men were not strangers to them. It wasn't difficult to understand the tableau presented to the soldiers. As they all stood peering down the hill, Hamish played his part with as much gusto as he could muster. 'C'mon. Let's go and look,' he said, and made a move as if to get off the horse.

'No....no,' said Angus, patting him paternally. 'Stay where you are and sing that song again.' He turned to the soldiers and confided. '*He's in love. Sing same song, since Loch Leven. The same old song, he even sings when he falls off horse. Hurt him. Still sing.*'

Angus turned to Hamish. 'Sing it, Hamish and I'll get you home.'

By the time Hamish began to croon drunkenly, 'My secret maiden, the girl of my heart', the first man was already down beside Dickens's body.

'*There's a body here. It's Dickens. Looks like the drunken fool slipped and fell. We'd better send a runner.*'

Angus belched over the nearest soldier. '*Have you Gaelic?*' The soldier wafted the stale breath away. '*Enough. Pooh! What a state you're in.*'

'*Enough ... Pooh ...,*' Angus echoed the words. '*I not in state.*' He shook his head. '*Boy in state. I take him home.*' Then he added. '*Do you like song? Beautiful she is.*'

Sergeant Tom Evans wasn't interested in hearing a lovely song. The discovery of Dickens's body was much more engrossing, a welcome distraction from a tedious day.

'I go now. Take him home?'

The soldier backed away from the smell of stale whisky and old sweat. *'Yes. Go on. Get out of here. We don't need you.'*

None of the men bothered to watch the two heading for the town. Hamish swayed on Pepper and Angus lumbered beside him, their voices blending discordantly over the hillside.

'Sorry, Angus,' whispered Hamish.

While Angus carefully guided pony and invalid along the track, Hamish managed to tell him what had happened. It was fortunate that Dickens had attacked him on such a bleak spot. Angus was sure the whole event had gone unnoticed. No crime was easy to hide when every glen had eyes that watched constantly, and saw even the stoop of the hawk upon the unsuspecting sparrow. 'Don't you worry, we'll get you safely home and then I'll get help for Ian Og.'

It wasn't long before a voice in the distance hailed Angus warmly. 'Well, Angus. I haven't seen you in weeks. I hope you'll stop for a while. Have you called up to see Eileen? She'll be pleased to see you again.'

Kenny Friend Cameron was standing in front of his home. Although he was well over the biblical allowance of threescore and ten years, he stood tall and proud. The blackthorn stick he carried was not to aid his walking, but to herd the black cattle that grazed beside the lochan nearby. Handsome in his youth, he still bore a fine head of wavy hair, although its whiteness betrayed his years.

The wee cottage at Lundavra didn't look large enough

to have contained Kenny Friend, his wife Eileen, and their eight children, but it did. The majority were now married and housed under other thatches. There were always plenty of children and grandchildren to gather at night around the fire. At this time of morning most of them were out, minding animals, hunting, or doing the many errands that filled their day. Angus was grateful there were few witnesses.

As the travellers drew near, Hamish's state became more apparent and Kenny lowered his voice. 'And we cannot be talking out here in the cold air. Come in for a rest.' Angus was already lifting Hamish from the pack saddle, and carrying him into the shelter of the house before he finished speaking.

'There's mischief afoot, Kenny, and I think we'll need some help.'

'That's young Hamish.' The older man was surprised. 'Whatever kind of mischief happened to him?'

'None of his own making, but I've got to get him home.'

'She'll not like it.' Even at this distance Lizzie's character was well known.

'No. The poor lad, he'll never be let out again. I wish Granny Morag was here.'

'That's your relative up in Glen Rowan. Aye, I've heard she has the gift. Some say she got it from the devil.'

Angus laid Hamish down on the earth beside the fire, before propping him up to give him a drink. 'That's nonsense,' he said. 'She's a great old character. She'd tell you all about the gift she has, if you lived close enough.'

Eileen, Kenny's diminutive wife, entered the house.

'I saw you arriving, Angus.' Then she noticed the young man on the floor and recognised the face that was smiling apologetically up at her. 'Hamish! What's happened to you?' In a moment she was down on her knees making soothing noises as she would towards any hurt child.

'Are you hungry?' she asked.

'I am a little hungry,' Hamish lied politely. In truth, he was famished. Eileen brought him a bannock, which he ate, and washed it down with some ale. He was now finding it hard to stay awake. Kenny and Angus were discussing what they could do, to help both Hamish and the missing Ian Og.

Angus had an idea. 'Sarah is down at The Weaver's and Hamish would be out of the way there, at least until he can walk home by himself.' He looked down and shook his head. 'He won't be doing much running or jumping for a while, but he'll mend.' His smile faded. 'Oh Lord. But how do we smooth things with Lizzie?'

'I'll get The Boy to do that,' said Kenny. 'He has a way with him.'

He went to the back door and gave a shout. Gago was aged twenty-five, with a wife and children of his own, but Kenny always proudly called him The Boy.

'He'll have her charmed soon enough. He'll tell her that Hamish has twisted his ankle during his search for Ian Og, and is a mite keen to have it seen to by your Sarah. She'll come to her own conclusions and will think he's not hurt at all.'

It wasn't long before the three were walking down the trail together. 'The Boy' Gago headed towards Maryburgh, while Angus and Hamish took the track west down to Achintore and The Weaver's house.

CHAPTER 10

THE RAUCOUS SHRIEK OF THE cockerel was never so welcome. Daylight meant the search was under way. It put heart into Sarah. She turned to the day's first task and began to stoke up the warm ashes.

It wasn't long before a pot of water was beginning to growl on the hearth. On the shelf near the fire sat two boxes of tea. The new tea was too precious to use, so from the other box she took a small handful of used dried tea leaves and threw them into the water. When it boiled she poured it into two bowls.

Remembering the treats that still lay in her bundle, she took out a green parcel of Glen Rowan honey, and added two large spoonfuls to Kate's tea. With both bowls steaming in the morning air, she carried them through the weaving room and knocked lightly on the bedroom door.

'Auntie Kate' Sarah whispered. 'I've made some tea.'

Kate was still sleepy, but sat up in anticipation of this rare treat. The two talked of home and Granny Morag, Kate's mother. Not only had she sent the honey, but from her bundle Sarah fetched a shawl that Granny knitted.

'She says it is for you because it would be bad luck to give it to an unborn child.'

Kate gratefully inspected the delicate cobweb knitting, and then draped the shawl around her shoulders. 'It's so long since I saw anyone from Glen Rowan. I'm so pleased you're here to keep me company. Everyone says the last two weeks are the worst. I'm sure when Ian Og gets here you'll settle down better.'

Kate chose to ignore the tears she saw welling up in Sarah's eyes and carried on. 'It's hard sometimes to be the only woman. I live with three men and they're all called Donald Cameron, but none of them goes by that name. There's my Donald. He's The Weaver. Very few people remember what his given name is.' She said it wistfully and then smiled. 'And you've met Donuill Dhu already. He's a great warrior, don't you think? There's too many at his home, so he came here last summer to help his uncle with the beasts. And the uncle is Donald Cameron too, but ever since he was little he has been called The Bull. He has a gift with cattle.'

While they sipped tea, Kate told Sarah of the daily routine. Normally The Weaver would be an early riser, so Kate would be early too. The click-clack of the loom could be heard even outside the house, so when it was working there wasn't much peace for anyone.

'Does he weave all the time?' Sarah wasn't sure how well she would cope with such a noisy contraption.

When Kate saw the dubious face she smiled. 'No. There's wool to buy and he visits the spinners. He visits the dyers too. You probably passed them as you came along the lochside. It takes a lot of wool or linen thread to make a piece of cloth, and he has to set it all up before he can sit down to work. It's wonderful to see the cloth coming from that machine. I'll show it to you after we've had some brose, perhaps with a wee bit more of this honey.' Sarah agreed. 'And oh!' she added. 'We must not forget Donuill Dhu.'

The byre outside was quiet. Sarah called out, but nothing stirred. She put the bowl of brose on one of the stools and was leaving the shed, when her eye caught a slight movement in one dark corner. 'There you are,' she said in greeting, but the shadow was gone.

Back in the house, Kate showed Sarah the loom. She could no longer fit behind it but pointed to skeins of wool. Different colours hung neatly on pegs set into the wall, and there were several bulging sacks piled in one corner. It was all very tidy, the spinning wheel, the reels for winding and plying the finished wool, the niddy-noddy for skeining and the pole for the flax.

It was a neat and tidy house, but Sarah also noticed it was a quiet house when The Weaver wasn't weaving. Although Glen Rowan was much smaller and off the main tracks, there was always something happening: children squabbling, men arguing politics or talking about cattle. Perhaps this was just a quiet day, but there weren't many people passing along the shore track either and no one had called in.

At home, Granny Morag always had plenty of visitors. People called to ask about dosing sick children or beasts, or how to sew up an ugly wound they couldn't manage themselves. Often they would stay to gossip, and sometimes there would be songs and stories, a little snuff, and tobacco for chewing or smoking. Beside the fire, they learned many stories of Ossian and Fingal, of the seal folk and the fairy king. If there were few visitors at The Weaver's house, opportunities to learn new stories would be rare.

While Kate was so big, she couldn't do much out in the field. With the men away there was little cooking to be done, and the two settled down to spin and knit and gossip together. It took a lot of work to keep a household clothed. Up in Glen Rowan, when there was plenty of wool, Granny often sold plied thread to the drovers that brought their herds over the hills. The men knitted as they walked. At cattle fairs, the socks and bonnets they knitted brought in cash.

As this day was mild, the two sat outside. Sarah was amazed at how her auntie spun the yarn so finely. Kate pointed out that she'd had much more practice. 'You'll keep improving,' she said.

Suddenly, she grasped her belly. 'Oh, God help me. It must be time, and The Weaver's gone.'

Sarah was stunned for a moment, but tried to keep her head. 'I'll send Donuill Dhu for the midwife.'

Kate waited for a few seconds before replying. 'No. It's not necessary. See, the pain's gone.' She straightened up. 'I'll finish this and then maybe I'll lie down. It's probably just a bit of cramp,' she said, as much to reassure Sarah as herself.

They were just back inside the house when the dog began to bark and then came lolloping round the side of the house. Donuill Dhu was close behind, reaching the corner of the track in time to accost the big man leading the garron.

'Visitors,' said Kate, waddling to the door.

'Uncle Angus!' yelled Sarah, running out, and when she saw that Pepper bore a rider she jumped for joy. 'You've got him.' Her heart released from its great burden rose to heaven and then hovered, but plummeted when she saw the rider's red hair. It was Hamish, and he wasn't looking good. A deep fear rose within her.

Angus called out, 'Quick! Give us a hand. He keeps fainting.' Prompted to action, Sarah scrambled to clear the table inside. Angus gathered up the lad in his arms. Donuill Dhu, mindful of his duty, took Pepper around to the byre while Kate went inside to join the others.

'He keeps going unconscious,' Angus explained, as he brought the lifeless bundle through the door. 'Where do you want him?'

Now with a job to do, Sarah found a new wave of energy and nodded towards the table. She looked down at the young man who had been so bright yesterday. 'What happened?' she asked. 'Was it the drovers? And where's Ian Og?'

Angus looked down meaningfully at Donuill Dhu. The young sentry was standing wide-eyed, inspecting the filthy specimen lying on the table, and it took Kate's sharp command to attract his attention. 'Donuill Dhu! Bring us some water.' He quickly left the room.

'He was following those drovers, up over the peat track near the Fairy Fort. Then a soldier attacked him. He had to kill him. By the sound of it, he was lucky not to have been killed himself.' Angus told them. 'It was that fellow Dickens you punched yesterday. Hamish cleared up the spot to make it look like he had an accidental fall.'

While they stripped Hamish, Angus told them all he had learned of the chase and the fight. Sarah began to unpick Hamish's tattered plaid bindings. Kate sat white-faced beside the fire. She waited till the pain passed, and went to fetch some old soft linen for washing Hamish down, strips for bandaging and an old leine belonging to The Weaver to clothe him, until he could dress himself.

Noting the older woman's discomfort, Sarah said, 'Auntie Kate, you go back and lie down. We'll be fine here.' So the woman withdrew to her bedroom, leaving the others to their task. When he returned with his pail of water, Donuill Dhu noticed Kate's absence, put down his pail and made his escape.

Sarah rummaged in her bundle and brought out two bunches of herbs that Granny Morag packed for her. One bunch went into a small pot of water which was then set upon the fire. The other was put to soak in a bowl.

She tried to clear her mind of the fact that it was her fault that Hamish was attacked while trying to help her. Somehow Dickens was seeking retribution against this brave lad. She nearly jumped out of her skin when Hamish spoke.

'Sorry, Sarah … I couldn't go any further. I'm sorry.' The voice trailed off again.

'It keeps happening like that,' said Angus. 'Probably best if he's out cold while we see what's going on.'

They had no difficulty finding the broken rib. Big red and purple blotches on the side of his chest signalled the damaged area. Fortunately the bone hadn't broken through the skin. It would be very sore, but it wasn't fatal. Sarah laid the healing herbs onto the bruised flesh and Angus rebound his chest. Hamish moaned his discomfort, but he was barely conscious.

The foot was more of a problem. When the makeshift plaid bandage was removed, they could see the brogue was held tightly by black and swollen flesh. 'I'll take the brogue off and you get it bandaged quickly. Maybe it'll settle down by tomorrow,' Angus said, and then added, 'If his mother sees it swollen, she'll be very annoyed.'

Remembering her own meeting with the dreaded Lizzie, Sarah shivered. 'She'll be annoyed anyway '

'Well, I was hoping that maybe I've forestalled her somewhat,' said Angus as he grasped the battered brogue and pulled firmly. Ignoring Hamish's groan, Sarah spread honey and the rest of the soaked herbs around the blackened foot, and bound it with Kate's linen strips. As she worked, Angus told her that Kenny Friend's son, Gago, was going to tell Hamish's mother that he'd fallen off a horse and wasn't badly injured, but wanted The Weaver's niece, Sarah, who was a healer, to take a look at it.

Sarah found herself smiling as they dressed Hamish in The Weaver's old leine. Angus laid him in the box bed. 'Lie still, Hamish. You're safe.' The voice comforted the youth, but he was obviously in pain.

Sarah brought some of the brew which was steeping at the edge of the fire. 'Let's try him with some of this. It's meadowsweet with a good dollop of whisky. It should knock him out.' Carefully, she began to spoon it into his mouth, and although he grimaced at the taste, he had soon swallowed several spoonfuls of the concoction and he lapsed into sleep.

Angus looked down at the lad and shook his head. 'He'll mend. I'd better be off and join The Weaver and his search party.'

With Hamish in good hands, there was no reason to stay. Angus took two bannocks from the iron girdle over the fire to keep him going, and bade Kate God's blessing on her confinement. He fetched Pepper, and with Donuill Dhu as his esquire for a few yards, he was soon cantering towards the town.

Sarah went to check on Auntie Kate. 'Would you like a drop of ale? Uncle Angus had the last of the bannocks, but I'll make more in a minute. There's plenty of broth, so you don't need to get up if you don't feel like it.'

'You're a good girl, Sarah. I think I'll stay where I am, but I don't know if I want any broth. I might have some ale and a bannock, when you've made them.'

Sarah returned a few minutes later with a bowl of ale laced with a generous splash of The Weaver's brandy. Kate was in pain again and clutching her stomach.

'Oh, Auntie Kate!' she cried out. 'Why couldn't you have said something? Uncle Angus will be too far away by now.'

'I didn't want to bother you when you were helping Hamish.' She relaxed as the spasm eased.

Sarah tried to sound confident. 'These things can take hours, can't they?'

'Oh yes,' said Kate. 'These things can take quite a time.' As if to give a lie to the words, she let out an involuntary groan as another spasm of pain hit her.

'We'd better get the midwife. I'll send Donuill Dhu to Mistress MacDonald at the dyers' burn. It won't take her long to get here.'

'Aye,' Kate said. 'That's a good idea, if you can get him to understand. He's not been further than the corner of the track since he's been here.'

'Still,' said Sarah sensibly, 'if he turns up at Mistress MacDonald's house, she'll soon work out that she's needed and who needs her.' Kate nodded her agreement.

Out in the byre there was no sign of the boy, except a half-carved wooden seagull lying on one of the stools, with new shavings beside it.

'Donuill Dhu! 'Sarah called. 'Donuill Dhu!' No answer, but there was a presence in the far corner. 'There you are' she said, firmly addressing the darkness. 'We need you to do a message for us.' There was still no movement. 'Come here,' Sarah insisted. 'Here!' She added firmly as if to a puppy, pointing to the spot in front of her. 'Yes here.' Reluctantly the shadow moved towards her.

'Do you know where the dyers' burn is?' There was no response. 'Dyers' burn, do you know it?'

Donuill gave her a tentative nod.

'Do you know Mistress MacDonald?'

He scrutinised the ground at his feet.

She repeated the question and there were several slow nods. 'Would you be able to go there for me?'

He nodded again and lifted his head.

'Could you ask for Mistress MacDonald? Can you remember that name?' She smiled encouragingly.

This time she got a tentative smile, along with the nods.

'Say the name,' she said.

'Mistress MacDonald.'

'That's right, very good.' Sarah was speaking like she would to a very young brother. 'Now, I want you to go and see Mistress MacDonald.'

'Mistress MacDonald.'

There was no nod this time, although the smile was becoming broader.

'Yes,' Sarah nodded her own head. 'It's on the track beside the loch. The dyers' burn, it's beside the loch.'

Donuill Dhu's head rose and fell in time with her own.

Sarah took his wrist and led him out around the front of the house. 'Go now, Donuill Dhu.' She pointed towards the town. 'Go and visit Mistress MacDonald at the dyers' burn.'

His smile faded. He looked at Sarah, at the outstretched arm pointing along the road and said, 'The dyers' burn?'

'That's right,' said Sarah. 'Mistress MacDonald. Now go.'

With the end of his plaid trailing and many a backward glance, the boy walked down the track in the direction she was pointing. Each time he turned she urged him on with a sweep of her arm. 'Go on,' she said again.

His progress was slow, but at last he was out of sight and she returned to the house. 'Phew! That wasn't easy. Donuill Dhu is on his way.'

Kate was in the main room tending to the iron girdle greasing it lightly with a piece of suet and preparing it for cooking more bannocks. 'I don't think so,' she said, pointing outside.

Thinking that the game he was playing with Sarah was over, the boy had sauntered back to the house. He hummed as he returned to his wooden seagull.

'No!' Sarah was disappointed. 'I'll go and try again.'

'I don't think it's worthwhile,' said Kate. 'He'll only stay away a bit longer. We'll just have to manage on our own.'

Sarah agreed. 'And if the baby is coming, it's going to take a while anyway. Mammy took ages, sometimes.' She hoped, with steely determination rather than confidence, that someone would pass by soon, before night fell. It was time to check on the other patient. 'He'll be very sore when he wakes up.'

When he awoke, it took Hamish a few minutes to work out where he was. Every part of him ached, but he felt safe and warm. It felt like he was in Heaven so he wasn't altogether surprised when the bed curtain parted and Sarah stood there. She was real enough, and gradually his thoughts began to assemble themselves. He remembered the fight, the dead soldier and Angus. But for now it was enough to see Sarah.

Thoughts of his mother kept surfacing, but Angus Sticks had said he was not to worry about that and he was content. Sarah put her arm around him as she held a cup to his mouth.

He was just beginning to sip the strange potion when there was a cry. He tried to move, but Sarah hushed him. 'Don't worry,' she said. 'I'll be back soon.' The bed curtain was closed and he drifted off again into a pleasant half world.

'Auntie Kate. Auntie Kate,' she called, 'are you all right?' but one look told her that Kate was not well at all. Sweat shone on her forehead.

'Would you prefer the brandy or whisky, Auntie Kate?'

'I think Angus's whisky will be stronger,' she said breathlessly.

'Drink this to begin with. You need it more than Hamish.'

Kate took the cup, drank it down then grimaced. 'Yeuch … I hate meadowsweet.'

The comment made them both smile.

'I hate it too,' Sarah laughed. 'But it's Granny Morag's favourite cure.'

Kate settled down for the night as best she could, and Sarah returned to check on Hamish. He was fast asleep. It was also best for her to get as much rest as possible so, exhausted, she sat down at the big table. Gradually her head lowered itself onto her arms and moments later Sarah was sound asleep.

CHAPTER 11

By the time he reached the flat ground beside Loch Linnhe, Alistair was whistling cheerfully. It had been an eventful couple of days. Not only had he discovered a secret way into the Black Fort, but he'd have pleasure telling Mary and Duncan Ban about the courage of their children. The boat was safe enough for the present, and the day's return journey from Keppoch Castle over the mountain track had gone well. There was plenty of time for his meeting with The Frenchman, and he still had several packages hanging on his saddle that he wanted to deliver.

The home of Dougall MacDonald of Kinlochmore stood near the head of Loch Leven. Several houses were grouped together, and the little clachan was an enclave of uncles, aunts, nieces, nephews and cousins. Alistair, like others, knew the family well, calling in from time to time, when he passed on the track to Rannoch Moor and beyond.

News was the main cargo for which travellers were welcomed, but Alistair carried more tangible messages today. There was tobacco of course for Dougall, but another package would cause a flutter of delight from his wife Sheila. She was partial to a drink of tea from time to time, and had a soft spot in her heart for the handsome young smuggler who often delivered it. She was not the only female in the house likely to put a welcome before him.

Dougall MacDonald was the proud father of four fine daughters and Alistair, a favoured nephew of the chief, MacDonell of Keppoch, would be a good match for any of them. Flora, the eldest, was eighteen. Lately there was some talk of young Andy Mor from Glencoe, but she told her mother the lad had big ears, which would make him unsuitable as a husband. Alistair Glic was a much more attractive prospect in her eyes. On this basis, her mother Sheila was looking forward even more to his visit.

Dougall himself, however, knew that whenever Andy Mor called to the house, there was no indication that Flora found anything at all detrimental in his appearance, while her own bloomed like the flowers which inspired her name. He smiled at her secret and would not betray it. Plotting and planning gave his wife much innocent pleasure.

The next two were not in any real danger of falling for the visitor. Kirsty and Jean were like twins, giggling together, sharing the daily nothings that only close sisters could find absorbing. Dougall knew that while Alistair's attentions to them would cause a flutter for a few days, he would treat them with cheerful accord, like he would any silly young lassies. Heather, though, was another matter. She was the youngest, and shy in Alistair's presence, but her shining eyes sometimes betrayed secret thoughts. Her anxious father wasn't sure that he wanted her to fall for this young buccaneer, and took comfort from the thought that there would be plenty of company drifting in as darkness fell. Dougall considered that, where daughters were concerned, there was safety in numbers.

Alistair was unaware of the stir his visits created. He enjoyed the attentions of the girls, and there would be good company around the fire that evening. No one would question when he excused himself to walk in the wood for a while. On his return, the girls would take turns to sit beside him or fill his bowl. Later, after an evening of news, stories and music, Dougall would accompany him to the byre where he might rest overnight.

It was in this frame of mind that Alistair arrived at the clachan. As he anticipated, the goods he brought were most enthusiastically welcomed and the girls made space for him to sit and share the evening broth. Soon others called in, making a cheery gathering. While the chores of carding, spinning and knitting occupied the women, men talked of the strange beasts to be found on the hill and in the loch. Old Uncle John had the reputation of a fine sennachie, and took little persuasion to speak of the clan's historic past. It was getting dark when at last Alistair excused himself to go into the woods.

Outside, his eyes soon adjusted to the failing light and he had no difficulty finding his way in the gathering darkness. The track was well known to him, but it would take a while to reach the usual meeting place. He kept an eye out for the lanthorn The Frenchman would have hung, to guide him towards the shelter of the ruins where they were to meet.

The rain had cleared and Alistair was concentrating on keeping his footing through slippery grass, when he heard the unmistakable sound of his own name, hissed in a low voice.

'Hello?' Alistair responded in surprise, looking round him to see where it had come from.

The voice hissed again. 'Down here ... It's me!'

Alistair couldn't believe his ears. 'Ian Og? It can't be.' The question carried clearly across the vegetation. 'What are you doing here?' He still couldn't quite see the lad and ducked down.

'Alistair ... Alistair!' The voice was hoarse but there was urgency in it.

'There you are. Pooh! You smell bad,' said Alistair, lowering his voice slightly.

'It's a trap. The Frenchman and MacCannie want to kill you. Don't go.'

Alistair was stunned, but realised something bad must have happened to Ian Og, and he wondered how this boy knew about his meeting.

'Quiet now. I won't go until you tell me what's happened.'

Knowing that his warning was finally conveyed, Ian Og gave way to the tremendous fatigue invading his soul, and fainted back into the mass of wet green bracken. He came around with a startled cry.

'Hush now. You're safe.' Alistair tried to soothe him, raising a cup of water to his lips. As Ian Og sipped, he felt the comfort of dry straw underneath him, and a warm blanket above.

'Are you all right?' asked Alistair.

'You didn't go, did you?' Ian Og flailed about and grasped Alistair's wrist spilling some water when he did so.

'No, no. You were a wee bit insistent, so I thought I'd better bring you back here to the byre and find out what was happening. There's still plenty of time.'

'It's a trap,' Ian Og was emphatic; concerned that Alistair might not have fully grasped what he was saying. 'You can't go.'

'I have to go. This man's important.'

'He's a spy. I heard it all. MacCannie kidnapped me and he was going to kill me and put the blame on you!'

It was a shocking and confusing story which emerged, sometimes painfully slowly and at other times in a tumble of words, but its importance was not lost on Alistair.

'Oh, that MacCannie's a whore's bastard!' He shook his head in disbelief. 'I never liked him. At least you're safe and no one knows you're here.'

As he talked, Alistair's mind raced as he tried to absorb what had been said, and consider what he should do now. 'We'd better not tell the MacDonalds. I'm sure Dougall is sound, but you never know. Strange things happen to families.' He held the cup to Ian Og's lips again.

Now that the full burden of his knowledge was passed on, Ian Og felt a surge of energy. He took the cup away from his cousin and drank greedily. 'I'm hungry. Have you got anything to eat?'

Alistair laughed 'I think you'll mend all right if you're hungry.' He rummaged in his sporran. Ian Og couldn't see, but he sniffed appreciatively. 'Is it a kipper?'

'Aye,' said Alistair. 'Will that keep you while I go and find out what is going on?'

It wasn't easy to protest with a mouthful of smoked herring. 'You're not really going to meet him, are you?' There was distress in his voice. 'MacCannie isn't far away, and he's got two men with him and lurchers. That's why I'm covered in deer shit, so the dogs couldn't track me.'

Alistair paused. 'You did very well to warn me, Ian Og. To be forewarned is to be forearmed and I'm going to go and take a look, and see who's there and what they're up to.' He handed Ian Og the cup. 'There's enough sweet water there to keep you for a while, but you'll need to keep hidden here till I get back.' Then his voice became more resolved. 'I'll have to keep my wits about me, but I'd like to see who else turns up. They'll pay, I promise you. The bastards! I'll make that renegade MacCannie suffer and the French traitor too.'

As Ian Og watched the dark silhouette disappear out the doorway, he wanted to cry out, 'Don't leave me alone!' but he held his tongue and the moment was gone.

Outside, at first Alistair was resolved to act as if nothing was amiss. He hurried towards the meeting place, a sheltered enclave of rock with trees all around. His steps slowed as he considered the setting. A man could easily be trapped there and harm done. From Ian Og's warning, it seemed that others were to witness the events. MacCannie obviously had a great evil in his heart.

As the dim light of the flickering lanthorn became visible, he ducked into the cover of some bracken, and circled around to a place where he could look down into the dimly lit clearing. There was no sign of The Frenchman, but MacCannie and Hugh were there. Alistair caught his breath. On the ground lay a young man and two sleeping lurchers tied to a tree.

From Ian Og's description, this must be the incompetent nephew, Ken. If he wasn't dead, he soon would be. Alistair was raised to be a fighting man and was no stranger to violent death, but the callousness of MacCannie against his own kin made his gorge rise. The hate within the drover must be immeasurable.

There was more than enough evidence to prove that Ian Og had not exaggerated. Alistair began to crawl away but a few yards later, he stopped. There was a faint whiff of tobacco. Inching forward he gradually made out the forms of two men, crouched like him within the shelter of the bracken and the trees. He wasn't close enough to see them in the dark, but they smelled of horses and leather, like soldiers. They must have been brought here secretly to witness his downfall. He wondered if The Frenchman was also hiding nearby.

He carefully circled around to avoid them, taking a different route, and finally returned to the cheery company back in the MacDonald house. He limped in, apologising for being away so long. Fresh stains of earth and grass on his knees looked as if he had tripped in the dark.

'It was careless of me. I'll just rest it for a while and it'll be fine.' He motioned away the fluttering assistance of Sheila. 'No, really. I've checked it and there doesn't seem to be anything damaged, just my pride.' He swiftly relieved her of the bandage she held and added. 'Mind you, I'll just take a couple of wee strips of that linen to keep it tight overnight.'

The company did not notice that his trip had taken some of the *joie de vivre* from the young warrior. He sang and laughed and listened to the stories, even telling some of his own.

A little while later, as Heather went around the company filling bowls with whisky, Dougall was a little alarmed to see that Alistair was marking his daughter with particular attention. There was a whispered conversation in which Heather became quite animated for a few moments. Then her face became expressionless. She finished pouring drinks for everyone and left the room. Dougall watched and waited. To his surprise, Alistair didn't make an excuse to follow her. He could have sworn that something had passed between the two, but Alistair stayed where he was.

Eventually Heather returned and Dougall could see no untoward signs between the two. She was in and out of the company several times. Alistair didn't make a move till the company was breaking up and, like any good guest, he was not the last to take his leave. He graciously thanked both Dougall and Sheila for their hospitality, and turned down the kind offer of company to see him down to the byre. Dougall watched him as he limped away, and told himself that with all his girls safely tucked up within the house, he was just being a suspicious old father.

In the byre the scene was transformed. A sleeping Ian Og still lay on the straw, but now he was clean and there was a linen sheet under him. The old animal blanket was replaced by another from the house. There was a comforting flicker of light from the remains of a suet candle set in a small lanthorn, and Alistair could see the boy's wrists were bandaged neatly. He guessed that a smear of honey had been used to dress the raw skin underneath. A fresh plaid lay beside the patient, and an empty bowl and spoon. Alistair was satisfied that he had chosen his accomplice well.

He kicked off his brogues and lay down in the straw. Ian Og awoke with a start. Then he saw Alistair and remembered he was safe. 'I never said my prayers,' he mumbled.

'I expect God will understand.' Alistair twitched the coverings. It was really only a token of trying to make the boy more comfortable. 'Go to sleep now and I'll get you to your auntie's tomorrow.'

As he lapsed back into sleep, Ian Og made an effort to speak. 'Heather' was the only word Alistair could make out as he settled comfortably on the straw.

At dawn Ian Og was the first to wake. Something dragged him from the depths of sleep.

'You're not going to just lie there are you?' It was the voice of Granny Morag. 'There's work to be done.'

Alistair felt a shake and woke up. 'It's me,' whispered Ian Og. 'I'm going.'

'What? What's going on?' Alistair sat up, trying to clear his head. He looked around him in the early light, to see what had disturbed the lad.

'It's MacCannie. I know he's near. I've got to get out of here.'

'Where is he? How do you know?'

Ian Og hesitated and tried to convey the intangible nature of his certainty. 'Well … I don't know. I just have a feeling.' But there was a tone of certainty in his voice which brooked no doubt.

'How near do you think he is?' Alistair had no qualms about accepting Ian Og's words.

'I'm not sure.' The lad pondered for a moment. 'But I should leave now. That man's out for blood. There's death around him. I can feel it. He wants more: my blood and yours too.'

Alistair was now well and truly awake. Intending not to scare Ian Og, he didn't mention the bloodied nephew. 'You can't go on your own.'

'Yes, I can and I must.' The words were not defiant, just a simple statement. 'You see, it was Heather. When we were talking last night, she said that her uncle James was very friendly with The Frenchman and she'd seen him sometimes with MacCannie. If they realise I'm here, they'll try again.'

'No, I don't think so,' Alistair said. 'Not under the noses of the family. We're safe here, but you're right. We've got to get ourselves away, and we must stick together. Separately they might get a chance to pick us off. Together, we'll manage.'

'Well,' said Ian Og. 'We will have to try. I'm stiff, but I've eaten and Heather gave me enough for the journey. She won't say anything because she doesn't like her uncle James, and she really hates MacCannie. She says he sort of pats her whenever he comes near her, and she doesn't like the touch of him at all.'

'Aye, he has a bad reputation around the womenfolk.' As he was speaking, Alistair made a decision. 'We'll get ourselves out of here now.' Searching in his sporran he found a little piece of paper. 'I'll leave a note saying that I have to leave early and get to Maryburgh, and thank them for their hospitality.'

Minutes later Alistair quietly led his horse with Ian Og on its back out of the shed, walked down the trail towards the Corran Narrows and slowly made his way towards The Weaver's House.

CHAPTER 12

THE MORNING WAS FRESH and sunny when Sarah went through to the wee bedroom again. All country children saw animals being born, and Sarah was at home when her younger brothers and sisters came into the world, but was rarely allowed near her mother at the time. Now she must be strong and sensible and try to think clearly.

'How are you doing, Auntie Kate?' she asked.

The face that looked up at her appeared very tired indeed. 'I'm fine but these cramps are sore.'

The baby was becoming impatient, but there was still time between pains for Kate to slowly waddle into the big room and fidget, to fetch and arrange the soft moss and linen that was saved for the birth. Sarah filled Kate's drinking bowl several times. Usually it held whisky. Sometimes honey was added, sometimes the meadowsweet. Once it held tea with honey and whisky. There were barley bannocks on the iron girdle and Sarah found venison strips in the cupboard. Lightly stewed, they would be a tasty addition to the menu. It kept her busy while Kate lumbered cautiously to and fro. Hamish wasn't forgotten either and he too shared tea, whisky and meadowsweet, but mostly he just slept, oblivious to events.

Kate was in the bedroom when she let out a sudden cry. Sarah rushed to help and found her with legs already drawn up. The steady intake of whisky dulled her discomfort, but the pains were finally merging into one. Sarah pulled off the bed coverings and put a soft linen blanket under her.

'Oh, Dear Lord, I think this is it, Sarah!' Kate cried out.

Neither of them had time to worry now. It was fortunate that the baby knew its task, and it wasn't long before the tiny head slowly emerged. Sweat ran down Kate's face as she strained to push the rest of the baby into welcoming hands. A new life was beginning. Sarah gently pulled away a thin cap of skin from the head and marvelled at the bloody, wrinkled but beautiful infant.

'It's a girl … She's amazing!' Sarah's voice was filled with wonderment. She lifted the baby for Kate to see.

'Oh, yes.' Kate's voice became soft and she began to cry. 'She's beautiful.' She stretched out her arm to touch one tiny hand. Her voice suddenly changed to a wail. 'But look! She's not breathing!'

'We have to turn her upside down,' said Sarah. 'I'd forgotten we have to do that and smack her bottom. We have to make her cry.'

'Oh no, don't smack her. No! She's so small and beautiful.' Kate sobbed. 'I'll hold her instead,' and she held out her arms.

Sarah had to be firm. 'We must smack her first.' She was scared that this slippery bundle might fall out of her hands, so she took one tiny ankle in each hand, gently up-ended the baby, and was immediately confronted with a problem. 'I don't know how to smack her. I haven't got another hand.'

Awkwardly she tried to lay her burden down again, but this wasn't easy as the head kept getting in the way. The baby suddenly coughed and spluttered for a moment, and then cried. Sarah managed to get the wriggling child face down, safely onto Kate's stomach where mother and daughter could cling to each other.

'Auntie Kate. What'll I do about the cord?'

'It'll have to be cut,' Kate said, and to the baby she added. 'Then you'll really be mine.'

'I wouldn't want to just cut it,' Sarah said. 'It if bleeds too much it might not be right.' She paused to think what Granny Morag normally did. 'I know. I'll use thread to tie the cord before I cut it. That's it.' She looked around her. 'I need a knife.'

'There's a good knife in the kitchen,' said Kate, 'or you can use the loom shears. There's linen thread there as well.'

Sarah went to fetch the shears. Returning to Kate she asked, 'How much space should I leave?' Kate was totally absorbed in her precious bundle, so Sarah plied linen strands together and made two ties on the cord and prayed that God and the angels would guide her hand.

'Auntie Kate, will I cut it now?' Kate was almost asleep.

'You may as well,' she mumbled. 'It's got to be done.'

Sarah took a deep breath and cut firmly between the two crimps. 'There!' she said 'It's done.'

It wasn't long before the afterbirth was cleared away and the bed tidied. Sarah left mother and baby to rest quietly together, and went into the other room to check on Hamish. He was still asleep, so with a big sigh of relief she filled herself a bowl of broth from the pot simmering over the fire. Sitting down at the big table to sup, she felt both exhilarated and exhausted.

It was late afternoon when the barking dog signalled a horse approaching. Sarah hurried out to greet the newcomers and give Donuill Dhu his war cry and praise. She couldn't believe her eyes when Ian Og jumped down from the horse's rump and came towards her with a cheerful yell, swerving around the defending gladiator and the barking dog. When Alistair dismounted, Donuill Dhu took the reins and led Alistair's horse to the byre.

Sarah's feeling of relief was somehow less than she had expected. 'Ian Og. You're here. What happened?' How did you get here?' He was safe but she was no longer the same person who had walked into the little town of Maryburgh a couple of days before. Her terrible fear for his safety since their first day in the town had since been overshadowed by other events.

'Alistair found me. They were setting a trap.' The words came tumbling out 'MacCannie kidnapped me, but I escaped! They were going to trap Alistair and make it look as if he murdered me.'

'He escaped.' Alistair's voice cut through the air and touched a strange chord within her. 'It was quite an adventure, don't you think?'

Adventure! Sarah was stunned momentarily. The word settled upon her like a bird of prey. These two were having adventures while she was worried sick. Somewhere within her a cauldron bubbled over.

'Adventure?' At last she managed to get the word out. 'Well, you can start a new adventure by fetching some water.' There was an empty pail near her, which she scooped up and threw at her hapless little brother. 'And you,' she said turning on Alistair Glic whose brown hair, sparkling eyes and cheery smile provoked rage within her. 'You can go and get Mistress MacDonald, the midwife who lives by the dyers' burn.'

'But …' Alistair, who anticipated at least a moderate welcome for bringing home the missing Ian Og, unwisely protested.

Somehow Sarah grew taller. 'No buts,' she interrupted. 'Get back on that horse and go now.'

She turned on her heel and stalked into the house. When she was in the bedroom she felt a sudden sense of relief overwhelming her. 'Auntie Kate, did you see? It's Ian Og. He's safe. Alistair Glic brought him. Did you see? They were on a horse. I've sent Alistair to get the midwife. He won't be long, I'm sure. Everything's going to be fine.'

'What was all the shouting about?' asked Kate drowsily.

'Nothing, I just got a bit carried away.' Sarah couldn't think how it happened. She was full of joy to see Ian Og again, and then she had just exploded. She was ashamed of herself. She'd been completely unreasonable. What must Alistair think?

'Thank God he's safe,' said Kate.

'I brought the water,' Ian Og's querulous voice came from the big room.

Feeling a bit foolish, Sarah came out to talk with him. He was peering cautiously into the weaving chamber. He looked small and vulnerable near the great machinery. Heather's neat dressings at his wrists and ankles emphasised his narrow bones, and he looked even smaller than she remembered.

'How is Auntie Kate?' he asked, his voice almost a whisper.

'She had a baby girl. I'm very sorry I shouted. I've been so worried.' She threw her arms around him.

'Oh Sarah, don't.' He pushed her away. 'You're being a bit funny.'

'I know.' She sniffed away the hint of a self-pitying tear. 'I've been so worried about you, and Auntie Kate needed me. Are you all right?' She drew him out to the big room and sat him at the table. A bowl of ale laced with whisky was set before him.

'Yes,' he gratefully gulped at the cocktail. 'My wrists and ankles are a bit sore, but Heather put stuff on them, and they're not so bad now.'

Despite all the other distractions Sarah heard gentleness in the tone of his voice. 'Heather? Who's Heather? How did you get away? Hamish went to look for you and he got set upon by that fat soldier I punched.' As she spoke she was automatically adjusting the broth on the hook over the fire before adding, 'And he killed him!'

'Is Hamish alright?' Ian Og asked.

'He'll mend. He's asleep over there in the bed.'

Ian Og rushed over and pulled the bed curtain aside. Hamish groggily opened his eyes. 'Ian Og! Thank God you're safe.' With a big smile he went back to sleep.

Ian Og watched him for a moment and whispered to the sleeping lad. 'Thank you, Hamish. Thank you. Yon Dickens deserved it.'

It wasn't long before the midwife arrived and took charge of Auntie Kate and her new baby. With relief Sarah returned to the big room and gave Ian Og a bowl of the simmering brose, and took away his empty ale bowl before preparing for any other arrivals.

On their way home, The Weaver, Angus and The Bull met Alistair leading his tired horse from the midwife's house. When they got his news that the baby was born, and that Ian Og was safe, they left him and galloped homeward with excitement. After they gave the war cry to Donuill Dhu, and he was satisfied, he went with The Bull to the byre, while the other two found a joyous group in the big room recounting in fragments the events of the past few days. The Weaver took no heed of anyone and rushed in to see Kate and the new baby.

Alistair was the last to arrive and before entering the house he found some feed for his horse. Inside the welcome was a cheery contrast to his earlier arrival. Angus, Hamish and Ian Og were at the table taking brose and Sarah was already laying out two bowls for him, one of soup and the other whisky.

Without a word Alistair devoured the food before him. Shortly afterwards, he sighed and wiped his lips. He filled his horn flask with whisky, picked up a couple of the warm bannocks and went outside to unhitch his horse.

He found Angus there waiting for him. 'Alistair, I just wanted to thank you for finding Ian Og.'

'Oh, no need. It was he who found me. He saved my life. MacCannie had set a trap. I was walking straight into it and Ian Og stopped me. The Frenchman planned it all. It seems he was always working for the other side. I promise you, Angus, when I find MacCannie and that Frenchman they'll pay dearly.'

'Traitors, the lot of them' said Angus shaking his head. 'We'll have to be more careful. Did Mrs MacDee give you a note when she bought the fish?'

'She did and I delivered it as instructed to that traitor The Frenchman on *The Leopard.*'

'It was not your fault, Alistair. We trusted him, but he didn't get it all. I also got some more news from her, so I must get to Dougie the Tanner as soon as I can.' As he turned his horse towards Maryburgh, Angus gave a wave to Sarah who stood at the door.

Now the conversation between the two was over, Sarah went over and joined Alistair as he adjusted his saddle and straps.

'Oh, are you going so soon?' Sarah spoke quietly.

'I'm afraid I must, Sarah.' He replied. 'I've got to meet up with the chiefs, Keppoch and Locheil, up at Keppoch Castle, and tell them of the events. I can't keep them waiting.'

'No. Of course not. But you must have thought I was very rude earlier. I'm really sorry. I was very upset about Ian Og.'

Alistair understood and he wanted to reassure her. 'Don't fret, Sarah. Ian Og is safe now. I'll make sure everyone learns about MacCannie and the other traitors. But now I have to go. There's talk among the chiefs that young Charles Stuart may be visiting Scotland soon, and there is a lot of work to be done.'

Before mounting his horse, he leaned forward and gently kissed her forehead. 'God keep you safe, Sarah. You have had a lot to bear on those young shoulders these last few days.'

She stood watching him until he was out of sight.

CHAPTER 13

HAMISH ROSE AND HOBBLED to the door to bid Alistair and Angus goodbye as they went on their ways. When Sarah suggested he stay a little longer while she cared for his wounds, he gratefully accepted. It would be prudent to stay another night and heal a little more, before facing his formidable mother. Within himself, he was pleased that his misfortune also brought him closer to Sarah.

Sarah herself was not too sure what to make of Hamish. He didn't behave like the boys did up in the glen. They treated her like one of themselves, and were candid in their assessment of her looks and personality. 'You're bonnie enough,' they'd say, and then add, 'but you have a fierce temper sometimes.' While there might be a hand held overlong at a ceilidh or dance, and maybe an attempt to snatch a kiss, or brush hands against her, the actions were generally awkward and a smack from an irritated Sarah would lead to a sheepish shrug from the culprit.

Having been kept on a tight leash by his mother, Hamish was cautious when it came to wooing a girl.

He didn't think he could say the sort of things Sarah might want to hear so he offered to improve her Scots while she was at The Weaver's house, and she was keen to learn. It would help her to understand the traders in the town. Mostly they dealt with the garrison, and the highlanders considered them to be hard bargainers. It was said that although they could speak Gaelic, they were more accommodating when they heard their own language.

Hamish had lived in Maryburgh beside the fort all his life. He was fluent in Scots, but being struck by Cupid's arrow didn't make him a skilled teacher.

'You can't just learn words, Sarah. You have to know about tenses.' He wanted the very best for his pupil.

This mystified Sarah. 'But I don't know about tenses when I'm speaking Gaelic.'

'Well, it's different when you learn another language,' Hamish explained. 'You have to know which verb to use.'

'But I don't know which verb to use now.'

'You do really, Sarah.' Hamish tried to explain. 'You see, you have nouns and verbs in Gaelic too. You just know which ones to use and when.'

That day, whenever Sarah was in the big room, Hamish took the opportunity to explain more about nouns and verbs and suggested many useful words to know. Sarah was somewhat relieved on the second morning when a wagon passed, heading for the fort. With foot and chest tightly bandaged, and with many thanks, Hamish took his leave.

When Hamish reached the town and climbed down from the wagon, with the help of a bent stick Sarah had brought out from the byre for him to use as a crutch, he was pleased to hear the news about Private Dickens. His dead body, complete with a tidy hoard of cash and some stolen food, had been brought back to the fort a couple of days earlier. There was no suspicion that it was anything other than a drunk falling, and he was buried that morning without a single mourner.

Having stopped to gather the gossip, Hamish knew there was no good excuse to delay going home any further. Leaning heavily on the bent stick, he limped home to face whatever histrionics Lizzie had in store for him, but even so, he wasn't prepared for the words that greeted him when he opened the door and blessed the house.

'Here at last, my hero son! Injured in his search for that young kidnapped boy! Look at him! My poor injured lad!'

This wasn't the welcome he was expecting and he waited quietly until Lizzie stopped to take a breath. 'Oh Mammy, I hope you haven't been worrying about me.'

'No. Of course not, my brave boy,' she said, throwing her arms around him.

Hamish was not fooled by his mother's bonhomie 'Have you got visitors, Mammy?'

'Oh yes. The blacksmith and his son came around to find out what happened to you. They heard that young Ian Og was kidnapped and you went searching for him.' She continued to speak loudly for the benefit of the visitors. 'You would have found him if you hadn't been stopped by that Angus Sticks. I'm sure he meant well to let you ride his horse, but it was a pity you were thrown off like that. 'The Boy Cameron, I think his name is Gago, told me all about it. Lucky you were near The Weaver's house and that girl healer, whatever her name is.'

As she stopped to take a breath, Hamish said, 'Sarah.' Abruptly she turned her head to look at him, and he added, 'Sarah MacDonell, down from Glen Rowan to help her Auntie Kate, The Weaver's wife.'

As his mother seemed to be lost for words, Hamish went through to the other room to thank the blacksmith and his son for calling. With an eye on his mother, he began to cough. Lizzie, wishing to look like the perfect mother, went to fetch some ale for him. When she was out of earshot, Hamish quietly told the blacksmith that he was sure there were likely to be a number of useful tasks in the forge he could manage immediately, despite his injury.

Although Lizzie returned promptly and set ale on the table, the blacksmith Cameron and his son Dougall were already standing, preparing to leave. He thanked her and said it was very fortunate that Hamish hadn't been delayed too long, because there were several jobs that urgently required completion, and even with his damaged leg her son would be most useful. With a grateful smile, Hamish ushered them out the door.

Once they were gone and the door closed behind them, Hamish sat and waited quietly as his mother poured out all her anxieties about his absence. Once she'd had her say, Hamish filled a bowl of ale for each of them and sat down opposite her. With a deep breath, he told her that, in gratitude to Sarah, he would be teaching her Scots so she could deal with the traders. It meant that when he found himself with some free time, he would visit The Weaver's house and teach her more. As she listened, Lizzie began to realise that his accident had somehow turned her boy into a man, and one who was taking quite a shine to The Weaver's niece.

A few days later, Hamish was able to borrow a horse from the forge and head down the Achintore road. When he reached The Weaver's house, he was surprised to find Alistair there, alone in the big room, sitting contentedly by the fire, puffing his pipe, waiting for The Weaver's return. Ian Og was out at the loch fishing. Sarah was with Kate and the sleeping baby, now named Isabel.

Hamish was curious to know why Alistair was there, and learned the local chiefs, Cameron of Locheil and MacDonell of Keppoch, were commissioning a consignment of new plaid from all the weavers in the area. Alistair waffled on about wishing to improve the general clothing of the men, and didn't mention a possible visit by the young Stuart prince.

In turn, Alistair wanted to know how the neurotic Lizzie had coped with her son's absence, and he was pleased to learn that she had apparently mellowed somewhat, and didn't object to Hamish coming to see Sarah.

When Sarah was free she came in to join them, laying ale and corn bannocks on the table and settling herself down. Hamish sat down beside her and from his sporran brought out some charcoal and wrote. '*I have a pen*' in Scots on the table and made Sarah repeat the words several times.

Then he began to explain that in the English and Scots '*I have a pen*' showed ownership and possession, while in Gaelic 'the pen is at me' showed relationship. Sarah felt learning this was useless. She didn't have a pen and didn't see how it would help her to get some fish or oatmeal.

Although Alistair looked as if he was taking no notice, Hamish's pedantic path to knowledge and Sarah's polite discomfort were hard to ignore, and at last he cleared his throat.

'Hamish, d'ye not think that maybe some practical examples might be simpler for Sarah just now?'

'But she has to learn the grammar.'

'Oh yes,' agreed Alistair. 'You're right. But maybe until she gets the hang of the grammar, a few phrases would improve her vocabulary.'

In his heart, Hamish knew his pupil wasn't progressing as well as she might, so reluctantly he nodded.

Soon Sarah was able to say phrases like '*Good Morning. I want fish*' and '*How much oatmeal do you want for it?*'

Although Hamish felt his position as instructor was somewhat undermined, he had to admit to himself that the lesson was becoming much more enjoyable.

With a wink at Hamish, Alistair began to widen Sarah's repertoire. '*The ugly soldier has a red nose.*' Sarah dutifully repeated this to get the accent right. Alistair nodded approvingly, and fed her the next line.

'*I do not love him,*' she continued. '*His bum is big.*'

Hamish's eyes grew wider as he tried to keep a straight face.

'*And it's hairy,*' Alistair added solemnly.

'*And it's hairy?*' added Sarah quizzically, sensing incongruity. 'What's *hairy*?' she asked and when her teachers convulsed in mirth she hit them both, but it was a good-natured protest, and soon the three settled down again to the lesson until The Weaver returned and claimed Alistair.

A few days later on his next visit, Alistair brought her a child's grammar book, and whenever there was an opportunity she began to look at the words. Hamish may have been interested in Sarah as a future lover, but Alistair treated her more like a favourite cousin. He liked being around her. One day he brought Ian Og a hard leather-covered wooden shinty ball and they tested each other's skill with two makeshift camans, bent sticks trimmed from nearby trees. Their contest was rough and loud, and all in the household came out to watch. Donald the Bull shouted unintelligible instructions through the toothless gap at the front of his mouth. Donuill Dhu jumped up and down with excitement, and then ran and cut himself a caman and went to help the younger player. Sarah, who was often minded to forget that she was nearly a mature woman, felt this was a bit unfair. She found another stick and went to assist Alistair.

It was quite an even scuffle between the four of them. Normally, Sarah would have been trounced by Ian Og, but a strong partner evened things up. After receiving a long pass she jinked around her brother, and made a quick swipe in the direction of the trees which had become their goal. The ball flew straight and true, but then the dog grabbed it and ran away, leaving the contestants to argue whether or not a moral goal could be allowed.

'Well played,' Alistair said to Sarah with a broad grin.

Despite yells, pleas, threats and commands, the dog could not be persuaded to release it, and the contest was abandoned with laughter. Eventually, that evening, Donuill Dhu found the missing ball in some long grass.

It was on one of his visits to The Weaver's house that Hamish learned which day Sarah and Ian Og would be travelling back to Glen Rowan. On his next visit he brought news that he planned to visit his own cousins living in nearby Glen Roy, and suggested that as his foot was almost better they might all travel together.

The following day, after gifts for the family in Glen Rowan were packed and fond farewells were exchanged, The Weaver brought the pair to Maryburgh where Hamish had been alert for some hours waiting for their arrival. Soon they were tramping steadily along the road, fort and town receding behind them.

At first the three walked abreast, but Ian Og kept questioning Hamish about the soldiers, The Weaver, the shinty players and other locals. With a sigh, Sarah adjusted her bundle and walked behind them half-listening, wondering how the two of them could find so much to talk about.

There was a long discussion about fights and skirmishes and the best type of weapon to use in different situations. Hamish was reluctant to acknowledge that the humble sling could prove as effective as the best claymore in certain circumstances, and Ian Og was not easily dissuaded from setting up a row of targets to prove his point. He spent the next hour picking up suitable stones and slinging them at trees or boulders along the way. He always hit his target. Both Hamish and Sarah agreed that, like David in the Bible, he would probably prove to be a deadly adversary given the chance.

Wishing to get home quickly, the three decided to take General Wade's straight new military road rather than the winding old track. This was not without hazard, and when soldiers came into sight, they ran off and hid until all was clear. Luckily there were not many patrols.

By the time they reached Wade's High Bridge over the River Spean, they were growing tired. Sarah didn't dare look down at the swirling water below, and carefully stepped along the middle of the bridge.

Ian Og and Hamish had no such qualms. 'C'mon, Hamish,' said Ian Og, walking ahead confidently. By the time Sarah reached the corner the two boys were nearly half a mile ahead.

She quickened her steps, glad that they would soon turn towards Glen Roy and Glen Rowan. Her bundle was heavy with the treasures gathered from her stay with Kate: Alistair's grammar book; a pair of good brogues and cloth from The Weaver; fine knitted stockings; a thick woven jacket to take home for her mother; and a sweet bannock for each of the young ones from their Auntie Kate. There would be much excitement over the gifts, especially the warm jacket for Mamma, who sometimes found it very cold working in the field.

It was in this buoyant frame of mind that Sarah saw Ian Og and Hamish nearing a group of soldiers. The post at Ruthven wasn't very large and the troops were changed from time to time. These looked as if they had just been relieved and were in holiday mood. They were ambling untidily along the road. A couple had muskets neatly over their shoulders, but others carried them loosely and, by the leisurely state of them, they were in no hurry to get back to Fort William in Maryburgh.

With moorland on either side of the road there wasn't much cover, but Hamish and Ian Og moved off the road to avoid them. One soldier looked over and called, *'What are you hiding, boy?'*

'It'll be contraband, I'll warrant,' said another.

Ian Og and Hamish moved steadily onwards through the heather, trying to get beyond the men as quickly as possible.

'Tell us, boy,' the soldier shouted. *'Maybe you've got whisky.'*

Ian Og just shook his head and kept his eyes on the ground ahead.

'A lad like you shouldn't be drinking whisky.' The voice carried provocatively on the wind.

The first soldier caught sight of Sarah. *'Here's one who'll be more civil.'*

'Aye, she looks as if she's got more than whisky in her pack.'

Sarah didn't know all the words but she caught the sneering tone. There were plenty of stories about what soldiers did to girls, and at the very least they would steal anything of value. She didn't hesitate and took to her heels across the scrubby heather towards the distant higher ground where there might be some cover.

There was a roar from the soldiers, and two of them threw down their muskets and jumped from the road into the heather and scrambled after her. The rest began jeering. *'She has you beat … you will never catch that one.'*

'I like a girl with spirit,' one of them yelled as he ran steadily after his quarry. Sarah had some advantage, being young and nimble, but she was tired and the soldiers were taller, with long powerful legs. She kept tight hold of the treasures in her cloth bundle. They wouldn't fall to those thieves without a fight.

The onlookers watched till hare and hounds were hidden by moorland tussocks. The corporal, with an avuncular shake of the head at the behaviour of his charges, fished out his pipe and lit it. *'Don't be long,'* he yelled. *'You can catch us up at the bivouac.'* Then he turned to his men. *'Let's move.'* And after a few more yells at their now distant colleagues, the straggling rabble sauntered on.

As she ran between the clumps of heather, Sarah tried to calculate how far in front the first birch trees were. She could also see rocks and boulders and hoped there would be a track through the rough ground. She tried to focus, but the pounding footsteps behind her meant the pursuers were gaining. Suddenly she stopped short. A slight dip and soft green mossy clumps ahead meant there was a large swamp of soggy peat, between her and the trees.

The soldiers were dangerously close, panting loudly as they ran. There was no time to think. She turned aside and kept on running, hoping the matted edge of the scrubland would be firm. Every muscle straining, she threw the precious pack away, but the soldiers did not pause and with a roar the man nearest dived forward, grabbing her ankle and yanking her down.

'Yes!' he yelled in triumph. *'I got her.'* As man and girl fell heavily onto the edge of the moor, the fragile overhang gave way and the two tumbled into the morass of the bog. His friend, who had stopped only yards away to rifle Sarah's pack, didn't realise the import of this till the triumphant yell of his comrade changed to a panicked shout for help. He dropped the bundle and ran forward.

When Hamish and Ian Og saw the two soldiers taking off after Sarah, they glanced briefly at each other, dropped their packs and ran as fast as they could. Ian Og covered the ground more quickly than the still handicapped Hamish. Fear lent them both wings and despite the greater distance they had to travel, they were near enough to hear the triumphant yell of the soldier, and then his frightened cry.

When they reached the scene, the floundering soldier was trapped to the waist in the soggy black liquid peat. He reached desperately for help towards his friend on the edge of the marsh. Neither gave any thought to Sarah. She was thrown further and more heavily out into the bog when her assailant fell onto her.

Although desperate, she tried to keep her head, knowing that to struggle would only worsen her plight. When Ian Og came rushing to her aid she was able to shout, 'The cloth … Uncle Donald's cloth!'

By the time Hamish caught up, Ian Og had fetched Sarah's bundle and was running back to her. 'Let those scoundrels have it.' Hamish said exasperatedly. 'Sarah's more important. Here, take my caman. We can nearly reach her with that.'

'Wait,' said Ian Og. 'We don't want the three of us in the bog.' He gestured with his head at the two men. 'And those two won't be quiet forever. Here … bring your caman and we'll use the cloth.'

The hard-cloth tartan would be more than long enough to reach the stricken girl. The two worked swiftly, tying one end firmly around the stick before Ian Og threw it with all his might out across the bog to where Sarah waited, up to her chest in the sludge and trying not to panic.

It only took a moment for her to grab the caman and the cloth and hold on for dear life. Hamish and Ian Og braced themselves as best they could on the edge of the moor, and dragged her inch by inch from the sticky bog hole. With a final slurp she was free and being swiftly dragged across the deceptive soft cushion of moss to the edge of the bog.

It was evident, from the intermingled cursing and praying from Sarah's attacker, that he was not having any success freeing himself. He soon found that floundering against the sucking peat caused him to sink further, and only when his colleague tried to reach him did he convulse with effort to grab the proffered arm.

His comrade was no less voluble with his cursing, as he kept trying to brace himself to reach out safely, but found the ground dangerously wet and fragile. When he noticed the others' success, menacingly he approached them.

'I'll take the cloth,' he called in Gaelic. 'Or the stick, that would do it.'

There are few stones in a peat bog. Ian Og had no missile for his sling except the hard shinty ball in his sporran. He began to whirl the sling in the air. It made the soldier pause. 'Keep back,' he said, and then turned to the others. 'Get going quickly.'

Hamish bundled the Weaver's cloth under his arm and made haste to help Sarah. She gathered up her precious bundle and they began to run from the scene, leaving Ian Og and his whirling sling. Although Ian Og had lived for only eleven years, in many ways he was wise beyond his age. He knew that these soldiers would have hurt his sister and thought little of it, but the mucky uniform they wore so carelessly deserved consideration. Dead or missing, revenge would be taken, scapegoats found, highlanders hurt. Alive, these two were much less likely to be a danger to any of them.

When the soldier saw the two leave with the tartan,

he sprang towards Ian Og who loosed the sling and caught him a sharp crack on the shin. As he cursed in pain and surprise, the boy bent down quickly, lifted the caman and threw it over beyond his adversary. 'There!' he shouted, turned and ran after the others.

CHAPTER 14

IT WAS GETTING LATE WHEN Sarah, Ian Og and Hamish reached Glen Rowan. On this the last stretch of the journey Hamish's injured leg grew tired. Their pace slowed but Sarah's heart no longer pounded. The evening sun still shone, and they should be safe now. The crystal-clear images of the chase were starting to blur in her mind, and the knot in her stomach was gradually easing. The only people they were likely to meet now were MacDonells, most of whom were close kin. Glen Rowan was a small valley, rarely appearing on military maps, and few soldiers noticed the rough track towards it when they passed through Glen Roy. Even fewer ventured along it.

As they walked, Sarah heard the clip-clop of a horse walking over stone. The other two also heard it, and started to move off the track, but Sarah instinctively knew there was no danger, and whoever was coming would not harm them. She made no effort to hide and kept on walking steadily up the glen. Now and again she took a look back to try and catch a glimpse of the rider.

At first, only the top of the leisurely chevalier's head could be seen, till he rounded a rocky outcrop. His face and shoulders caught the last rays of late sun, and there was no mistaking the jaunty angle of the bonnet or the rich brown hair.

'It's Alistair,' Sarah called to the other two.

'So it is,' Ian Og jumped up and down with anticipation. He turned to Hamish. 'I wonder where he's going.'

Hamish said nothing for a moment, his lips pursed in thought. 'Aye, I wonder.'

At last, horse and rider were in plain view. Seeing the three ahead, he gave a cheerful yell and kicked the laden garron into a slightly faster walk. Once alongside Sarah, he brought the horse to a stop and looked down at the peat-and-moss streaked girl.

'You look as if you had a hard day.' He dismounted and hooked her bundle onto his saddle before beginning to walk beside her. 'We may as well let the horse carry that.'

'Thank you,' she said, with a grateful sigh. 'Indeed the day was hard.' Then without further elaboration, she asked. 'Are you coming to visit us?'

'I have this load to deliver to Angus and I thought I'd maybe stay in Glen Rowan tonight.' He paused. 'Do you think your Mamma would be pleased to see me?'

It was a rhetorical question. Alistair knew well that he would always be sure of a welcome from his auntie, although it was a long time since he'd visited the glen. Sarah was delighted. Hamish was already invited for the night, and with Alistair there as well she felt the ceilidh would be complete.

She beamed as she replied, 'Oh yes. Grannie Morag was to brew some of her heather ale for us on our return. It must be well ready by now.'

'I've had her heather ale before. It's famous.' He

paused a moment and then asked. '*Are you speaking Scots yet?*'

'*I have a little Scots, sir,*' she replied earnestly and added in Gaelic 'Still not very much, but I'm grateful for the book. I'll study it more at home and Ian Og says he'll help me with the letters, although he says girls don't need to be reading.'

'Aye,' Alistair nodded. 'I don't think he's very keen on his own lessons and he wouldn't like to be beaten by you.'

'Hamish was encouraging him with his Latin,' Sarah sighed, 'but he'd rather be out on the hill catching animals for the pot.'

'He'll not go hungry, that one.' It was a compliment. 'But he is the oldest boy and he needs to get some education, too. I never cared much for the lessons myself until I saw a bit more of the world, then I wanted to learn everything.'

'Well, I'd like to learn to read.' Despite the grammar book in her pack, Sarah wasn't confident she could manage such a daunting task.

'It isn't that difficult, really. Just keep practising,' Alistair assured her. 'If you learn I could write to you.'

'You wouldn't, would you?' This was too much to hope for!

Alistair didn't seem to realise how much this would mean to her, although the offer was genuine. 'Yes. Honest, I promise. If you learn how to read and write, I'll write to you.'

'And tell me about the places you go?'

'I will, if you like.'

'Oh yes, please! I'd like to hear all about your travels.'

The other two stopped and waited for them to catch up. Ian Og was bubbling over.

'Did she tell you what happened with the soldiers? We were very lucky to get away.'

Sarah shook her head at her brother's enthusiasm and explained to Alistair. 'Some soldiers chased me into the bog today and that's why I'm ...' She didn't need to finish the sentence as Alistair looked her up and down, and nodded his understanding.

'And Ian Og rescued me,' she added. 'I'm really grateful, but he's never going to let me forget it. And it was all down to the shinty ball.'

'And the caman I used as a crutch,' Hamish added.

'Don't forget my sling,' Ian Og was triumphant.

Alistair then heard three versions of the fateful encounter with the soldiers, before it occurred to Ian Og to ask, 'What are you doing here Alistair? Are you visiting Mamma?'

'Yes, I'm looking forward to that.'

'Great!' Ian Og bubbled up. 'It'll be a wonderful ceilidh here tonight. Won't it, Hamish?'

Hamish's enthusiasm wasn't so warm. 'Oh aye, the craic will be good, I'm sure.'

Alistair didn't appear to notice any irony in Hamish's tone. 'I'm glad I caught up with you, Hamish. I was hoping to have a word with you.'

'Me?'

'Aye, before the others get here.'

'What others?'

'The locals, they all want to see the three of you and hear about your adventure. I was just about to tell Sarah that I have to be going over the Corrieyairack tomorrow and I need some local information.'

'I'll go with you,' Ian Og chimed in. He could always smell an adventure.

'Wait a minute, Ian Og. There would be some serious

questions asked if I agreed to that,' laughed Alistair. 'You might be a bit young for this sort of caper.'

'I am not,' Ian Og defended himself stoutly. 'I'm as good as anyone.'

'I'm not saying you're not. You're just too young. The rest will be older. But I do have a job for Hamish if he'll take it.'

'If he can go, why can't I?' Ian Og persisted.

'Nobody says he's coming with us.'

'That's enough,' Sarah grew impatient with her brother. 'Take a telling. Even if Alistair said you could go, it wouldn't be up to him anyway. Dadda and Mamma would have a lot to say if you were hiking all over the mountains, getting in the way.'

'I wouldn't be getting in the way. Would I, Alistair?' There was pleading in his voice. 'I wasn't last time. I saved you from that devil MacCannie and the Frenchman.'

'No, you weren't in the way, and yes you did.'

That was what Ian Og wanted to hear. He turned to his sister, triumphant. 'See? Alistair says I wouldn't be in the way. Anyway, I wasn't too young to rescue you from those soldiers.'

Sarah turned to Alistair and smiled. 'I said I'd never hear the end of it.'

Alistair realised the conversation was leading into awkward territory. 'Ian Og, we know you're brave, but the planning isn't done. I need to get some information from Hamish.' He looked down at the glum face. 'You will just have to be patient. There will be other times.'

'Honest?'

'Yes.'

'Do you promise?'

'I promise.' Alistair was smiling at the youngster's

enthusiasm. 'In the meantime, would you like to ride?'

'Would I?' Hardly had the words left him before Ian Og was up on the back of the little horse waiting for Alistair's nod.

'Wait a moment. We'll put the other packs on as well.' He added Hamish's pack to the saddle. 'There now, you can ride home if you like. Tell them we're coming.' With a smack of encouragement on the rump, he set the beast and boy on their way. It wasn't long before Ian Og rounded the turn over the hill, and disappeared with a wave.

The track was still too small for three to travel abreast, and Sarah again found herself following the leaders. She didn't think it was intentional but Alistair and Hamish kept lowering their voices, and she could hear only occasional words. Mostly it seemed to be about cattle. A herd was due through the pass, and there was word that some mischief was intended. She heard the name MacCannie. Badenoch was mentioned too. Sarah knew there had been trouble there lately, with armed gangs on the prowl. Hamish kept nodding in agreement with Alistair. She heard him say, 'Me? I'd like to do that.' Then it was Alistair's turn to nod enthusiastically. With each step, the two left her further behind. It seemed they had forgotten all about her.

At least without her pack, the going was easier and there was only half a mile to go. As she plodded on, she started to feel a bit sorry for herself, until she heard a steady clatter of hooves behind her again. Then the comforting aroma of Uncle Angus's tobacco wafted towards her on the breeze, and she stopped to wait for him.

CHAPTER 15

WHEN IAN OG ARRIVED ON Alistair's horse, it seemed that all of Glen Rowan and quite a few from Glen Roy were waiting to greet the travellers. The young ones had spent days gathering wood for a huge bonfire, and with his arrival they rushed to light it. The celebrations had begun. Grannie Morag's ale was broached and Angus's whisky poured.

Shortly afterwards, when Alistair and Hamish, still talking earnestly, trod steadily up the track, they were greeted with cheers. Anghie and the twins didn't know either of them, but cheered with the rest. They soon learned that Alistair was a sort of happy cousin, a naughty young nephew of Mamma and Dadda, and that Hamish was his blacksmith friend.

The company made a big fuss of the pair, and Alistair was his cheery self with his usual banter and gossip. From time to time he was approached by men, sometimes two or even three at a time, and quiet conversations took place.

By the time Sarah and Angus reached the croft, the

ceilidh was in full swing. Sarah's tiredness evaporated when she reached the welcoming throng and began to greet everyone. There were many questions; some wanted to know about Peter and why Sarah and Ian Og came to his rescue. Others wanted to hear about Kate's confinement, while the little ones asked about Isabel, their new baby cousin.

The men were interested in Ian Og's capture and wanted to hear of his escape. One or two knew of Alistair's close encounter with the traitor Frenchman, but first, everyone wanted to hear about the day's adventure with the soldiers, and the dash through the heather. Sarah's rescue from the bog in the nick of time was repeated over and over. There were several of Hamish's own cousins present, including Lachie, his favourite cousin. As they chatted together, they found themselves being surrounded by a group of mostly female admirers.

Dadda and Uncle Roderick were supposed to be in charge of the cooking at the bonfire. Mamma and Grannie Morag were on hand to give directions. So far there were no disasters. Both men were known to forget domestic responsibilities when social ones called for a song, a recitation or a story. The brothers were easily distracted by the company around them. With another sup or two of whisky they became more of a hindrance than assistance with the food.

Sarah smiled when she saw her dear Dadda and uncle waving glowing sticks from the fire, both grinning broadly, proud of their culinary efforts. Two hens were roasting on the embers and a couple of salmon were laid out on hot stones. It was obvious a sheep had been sacrificed too, with slices of mutton grilling over the fire.

Mamma, now very pregnant, was resting on a chair, and beckoned Sarah over. Grannie Morag filled a bowl with broth for her. Grannie wasn't one for great shows of affection, but she beamed to see her favourite granddaughter return home.

'I'm glad you're here at last. It'll give me someone to talk to again. Get this broth down you, and the twins will bring you ale and a stool.'

Sarah smiled across at the older woman, and then down at wee red-haired Morag, who willingly fetched a stool, while Eileen brought some ale. It was a relief to sit down properly for the first time that day, and give her bruised feet a rest.

Cousin James the Lion sat on a stone with his back to the company, and on his fiddle he played lively music, which rose through the babble of cheery voices.

His assistant, on the other hand, wasn't shy at all. Wee Anghie, Sarah's nine-year-old brother, was proving to be quite a musician on his whistle, despite stopping regularly to take a mouthful of bannock or meat, and a sup of ale. He longed to get a chanter when circumstances allowed, but such things were costly to buy and hard to make, even if they had any crab-apple wood. Dancing hadn't begun yet, but eager toes were already tapping beside the fire.

As Angus led Pepper around the festive bustle towards the byre, there were handshakes and hugs, nods and smiles and a few words, but his first thought was for his pony. 'I won't be long,' he told everyone.

On seeing him, Hamish excused himself from his admiring relatives and followed. Ian Og was already outside the byre helping to gather up small packs to bring inside, leaving Angus to attend to the patient Pepper. It wasn't long before Alistair joined them.

'These are the extra supplies you wanted,' Alistair gestured towards two sacks in the corner, where he had put them.

'Good man!' Angus was delighted. 'I'd better be doing something about that now.' It was whisky-making time again, and while Pepper always carried a good load, Alistair's cargo would ensure a full batch. It was a vital harvest in these frugal days.

'I've had a word with Hamish,' said Alistair. 'I hoped he would be fit for tomorrow, but he's still recovering from the run-in with Dickens, so I thought it might be a good time for him to learn how the whisky is done. He'll never get a chance at home.'

Angus nodded. 'Well, that's certainly true, but Ian Og is my apprentice now. He's nearly as good as you were.'

'Aye, there is a knack to doing it well, but it occurred to me that Ian Og might take Hamish's place with the cattle drive. It'll keep him busy and he'll learn some of the drove roads. I still have to check with Dadda but it's an opportunity to be one of the men and not far from home. What do you reckon?'

'Well … See what Dadda says. He'll have the last word.'

Picking up his pack, Alistair turned to leave. 'Now, I'd better get out to the music. There are plenty of pretty lassies here who need a dance. Besides, I want to give Sarah's mother Mary a present.' He untied the top of his bag and showed Angus the contents. 'Do you think she'll like them?'

'I've seen these before, but not often.' Angus put his hand in and brought out a knobby brown lump covered in earth.

'Do you think she'll give them a go?'

'I don't see why not. She'll plant whatever might help with getting us fed. It's getting near her time, so if she's not up to it I'll bet you that Grannie Morag will. She's game to try anything new, that one. Have you tasted them?'

'Yes, but only once,' Alistair said.

'Were they nice?'

'They were different,' Alistair mused on the point. 'The outside was kind of rough, but the inside was a bit like a soft white bannock.'

'Ach well. It's something for the women to talk about.' Angus returned the precious potato to the bag with the other two.

Outside, the party was in full swing. It didn't take much to tempt the dancers, and when Dadda and a very pregnant Mamma gently led the Glen Rowan reel, it drew nearly everyone to watch or take part. In the crowd, Angus found Ian Og amid a cheery group of cousins and beckoned him with a slight tilt of his head.

'Go and find Hamish,' he murmured. 'Bring him back to the byre and we'll get those sacks up to the burn now.'

By the time the pair got back, Angus was already hefting two big sacks, one on each shoulder and he nodded towards the two smaller sacks. 'Bring them along.' He strode off up the track. Ian Og and Hamish exchanged looks and then grappled with the other sacks and hoisted them over their shoulders, before following, nearly bent double, into the darkness.

At the burn there was a pool hidden by rocks where the sacks would soak up the clear mountain water overnight, out of sight of any chance passer-by.

'Tomorrow,' said Angus, 'you'll both come with Pepper and me as far as the hideout and Ian Og will show you how to spread out the grain, Hamish.'

'Right,' said Ian Og.

'And Hamish, you are going to be in charge of this, so pay attention.'

For Ian Og this was a surprise, but before he could ask why he was being sidelined, Angus turned to him. 'And you are to come on the cattle drive tomorrow. Time you met the drovers and saw what goes on. It's not always easy and the sooner you learn the better, but till then we have to make sure Hamish understands the job.'

On their way back to the bonfire, Angus told Hamish about spreading all the grain in an even layer over the linen sacks on the floor of his hideout. More importantly, the task called for caution and circumspection, so that no one would spot his destination. There wasn't anyone in the glen who would wittingly give him away, but wagging tongues and prying eyes could cause trouble.

Back at the ceilidh, James the Lion was taking a rest, and Cousin Marianne was singing. Her clear voice rang out sweetly across the darkness. It was a famous love song and everyone joined in the chorus. Grannie Morag was persuaded to give her recitation of the Battle of Locheil where the MacDonalds had routed the upstart Campbells and driven off their cattle. More stories and songs arose from the company, until little by little the assembly dispersed. The raucousness of the night dwindled, and those not already asleep were in quiet discussion with Alistair, about the cattle drive on the morrow.

To Grannie Morag's relief, Uncle Ranald was to stay with the women in the croft. She was always very protective of her first-born son. The simple soul that he was, he responded by being obliging and loving in return. He was happy to be 'in charge' at the croft. This fiction would be maintained by everyone throughout his reign, and even the seven-year-old twins, Eileen and Morag, would seek his opinion about all manner of tasks. The answer was generally the same: 'What do you think Dadda would do?' and then 'Well, I think we should do that.' Perfectly satisfied with himself, he would go about his own tasks, generally gathering peat, or fetching wood, which he piled neatly beside the byre.

Next morning, when Alistair roused the men, there were plenty of sore heads, including his own. With work to be done making whisky, Angus Sticks, Hamish and Ian Og rose earlier than everyone else, and led Pepper to the burn pool and loaded her with two large sodden sacks. Although much excess water drained off, this was still a heavy burden for a willing beast, so Angus carried one of the smaller sacks, and together the boys carried the other.

They climbed steeply for a while and stopped at a spot not easily seen from any direction. Angus's hideout nearby was hardly visible. Dug back into the side of the hill with a turf sod thatch, it provided shelter from the rain and some defence against birds and mice, who could make short work of tasty grain. Angus laid down his own burden and unloaded Pepper.

'Now remember what I said: a nice even layer and check it every day, preferably twice a day. You show him, Ian Og.'

When the soaked oats and barley were spread out and left in the dark, they would start to grow, otherwise the drink would be poor stuff, and only fit for beer.

'And then you can go and make a start on the kiln,' he added. He knew Hamish wouldn't be able to achieve too much, but Angus would be happy enough with any start made on the work

CHAPTER 16

IN THE COOL DAWN MIST JohnJoe Chisholm could hear the dull sound of grass ripping, rough mastication and the flatulence of contented cattle. Progress was good from Aberchalder but there were many miles before them, and the herd couldn't be allowed to rest for long. A steady pace with regular grazing breaks was ideal to bring the cattle to market in prime condition.

Ahead lay the Corrieyairack Pass. It was steep but there was fodder aplenty to maintain bovine energy, while they walked about ten to fifteen miles each day. The cattle were settling down, but there were tracks to tempt a curious animal to wander, and a skilled drover needed eyes in the back of his head. Over a hundred beasts could be a handful even with three men to help, and the pass was always risky. It would be a relief when his brother Kenneth joined him today with his herd. There would be more eyes to keep watch.

JohnJoe and his older brother Kenneth had been droving cattle since they were old enough to prod wild-eyed mountain beasts with a hazel switch, and tramp barefoot alongside their father, on the great summer treks from Strathglass to Crieff, through the grey hills of Badenoch and Lochaber and down the steep valleys to Bredalbane.

Ever since then, each of them drove cattle almost every year, sometimes together but not always. One time Kenneth broke his leg and despite the best efforts of the bonesetter, he couldn't even hobble for several weeks. He still limped to this day. Another season JohnJoe himself was close to death with a fever for nigh on three months, raving and sweating in his sick bed, until the cloud in his eyes gradually cleared and he knew his family again.

The two brothers had founded dynasties of their own after their father died. They trained their sons in the drover's way. Neither JohnJoe nor Kenneth would have used the word 'art', but if pressed they were likely to agree that the work held mysteries that could not easily be taught. It called for experience; an eye for the weather, an ear for the cattle, and a nose for the land about them. High integrity was necessary too, and both men were trusted and respected by whole communities across the Great Glen. Their work was to drive cattle safely to the trysts at Crieff or beyond, sell them for the best price available, and return with cash, promissory notes or grain to keep the highlanders fed during the winter.

Kenneth was bringing a herd from Strathglass, passing near Fort Augustus at Kilcumin on the old route, and then up the valley to join his brother's herd from Sheil and Loyne. There would be good grazing at this time of year. In some of the lowland areas where pasture was becoming scarce landowners wanted payment, so an early herd had a better chance to use any free grazing that was still to be found, and keep down the increasing costs of the drove.

In their father's time, all the common land was freely available to herds. Since then, wee hamlets along the way became towns, with grand mercat crosses in the squares, where people could meet or trade goods. Fat bailies in fine linen and the magistrates of the day knew well how to turn a pretty penny for grazing on their land.

There were other hazards to be faced before reaching the lowland landowners. It was more than ten years since Rob Roy, drover-turned-raider, had retired to Balquhidder, but cattle stealing was still rampant. The Corrieyairack Pass lay close to Badenoch and Lochaber. The clans there were hardly tamed yet, and the cattlemen would need all their skill and courage to meet and overcome any raiders they met along the way.

Neither of the brothers looked like a hero. Small and taciturn, they rarely spoke more than was necessary to encourage their charges on the trail, but a man would have been foolish to take their slight stature for weakness, or their silence for slow-wittedness. While quiet tact and cautious diplomacy were their main weapons, each carried an armpit knife under his jerkin, a sword and a charged pistol in his belt.

Their men carried swords too, and stout cudgels. There was no bluff in their defence against marauders. They spoke truth, fought to the death if necessary, as more than one thief learned before drawing his last breath. The rewards were few. The life was hard, but honour was mighty and cattle was the lifeblood of the community they served, the difference between food and famine for the coming winter. JohnJoe told his men to round up the herd and head up the glen.

Back in Glen Rowan, Angus found a willing assistant in Hamish, and was giving him last-minute instructions for sprouting the grain, before mounting the ever-patient Pepper, with Ian Og riding double. Even as they rode away, Angus turned to call out another suggestion, but Hamish was already bent to his work, setting out the linen sacking. Angus smiled and rode off up the hill, shaking his head benevolently at the eagerness of the youth. Dadda and Roderick joined them, riding their own horses.

Over in Glen Roy, Angus and Ian Og gathered more men, and quickly picked up the trail of Alistair's party who were mostly on foot ahead. At the top of the glen, where the two mountain rivers met, they took the left fork to come down towards Culachy, where they would meet up with the herd later in the day.

Alistair's men were veterans of regular cattle raids. In days gone by, MacDonell was a name to put fear into cattle owners. There were still plenty of local men who considered other people's livestock a fair means of increasing one's siller, but times were changing, even in the Highlands. By the time of the 'Fifteen' rebellion twenty-five years earlier, the government was already taking an active interest in the behaviour of the clansmen.

Chiefs who rarely gave any consideration to neighbours found themselves being held in check by a foreign government in Edinburgh or London, which ruled with financial promises, backed by a standing army quartered at forts throughout the glens.

The chiefs in turn commanded tacksmen and other tenants, with dire punishments for theft or disloyalty. Cattle and sheep stealing became rarer. The likelihood of being caught was low, but for the MacDonells this venture was not to be a raid on JohnJoe's herd. Their mission was to protect it.

The news that MacCannie and his men were near and causing trouble put all the drovers on alert. Glengarry, chief of the other local branch of MacDonells, made it known that he would consider it a favour if the animals from Sheil and Loyne were allowed to pass without trouble through the Keppoch area of influence. Such a request was unusual, but it would be a point of honour to ensure that JohnJoe and his brother came to no harm on any MacDonell territory.

When Alistair and his men reached the valley, they could see from the hoof marks in the rough ground and trampled grass from both cattle and horses that the herd had already passed. Fresh dung was evidence that the beasts were not far ahead. A few scattered cows grazing at leisure could be seen.

'There they are,' said Ian Og as he climbed slowly off Angus's horse. After the night's revelry and little rest, the day was beginning to take its toll.

With a noisy inward draw of his breath, Angus shook his head. 'Too late,' he pointed to where the hoof slots were deeper and spaced at longer strides. 'These are only the laggards which weren't driven off.' He turned to a couple of the men. 'You'd better round them up.'

Alistair reached down and gave his arm to Ian Og. Spurring his horse onwards, he shouted back to Angus and the others 'C'mon', and began to race up the rough track.

They passed the first two drovers lying where they had fallen, but didn't stop. The men behind would take care of them. The third was sitting a few yards further on, clutching a leg that lay awkwardly on the grassy track. 'Dung of the Devil,' he shouted at them as they pulled to a halt.

'Not us,' said Dadda, who had caught up with them. He slid down off his horse. 'We're here to help.' He looked at the leg. 'Broken?' he said, and when the man nodded in reply he added, 'The bonesetter will soon see to that. I'll just pull it a bit straighter now.'

As the man grimaced in pain, Alistair shouted, 'Where's JohnJoe? Did they take him?'

'I don't think so.' The man nodded up the glen. 'He'll be up there somewhere.'

A few minutes later they found JohnJoe, blood streaming from a gash on his head and still waving his discharged musket. He turned abruptly, brandishing his sword to face this new danger. When he saw who was there, he shouted. 'Alistair Glic! Is this your work?' Then his legs seemed to give way and he collapsed.

Swiftly, Alistair was down beside him. 'No, JohnJoe, not at all.' He reassured the drover. 'We came to meet you. Give you an escort, but you were quicker than we thought. Have you any idea who attacked you?'

'Not sure,' JohnJoe sighed. 'I think it was MacCannie and his sons.'

'Aye. We know he's in the area.'

'They were hidden and just came out of the ground.' He raised his arm. 'Then they started yelling and screaming at the beasts.'

'Aye, they had plenty of cover around here to hide in wait,' said Angus.

'Which way did they go, JohnJoe?' Alistair asked.

'What about the others?' JohnJoe remembered his men.

'They'll mend,' said Alistair grimly. 'Which way?'

JohnJoe collected himself. 'East,' he said and pointed towards the track.

Angus nodded. 'Aye, if they get through Glendoe and down into Stratherrick, they could lie up for months and no one would be any the wiser. At least their tracks won't be difficult to follow.'

Looking at the churned-up ground, Ian Og nodded in silent agreement.

'How far are they ahead d'ye reckon?' Alistair asked JohnJoe.

He thought for a moment. 'They're about a quarter of an hour, or maybe less. Most of them are on foot and the cattle won't keep it up for long.' The man was exhausted with all the talk and dropped his bloodied head into his hands. He looked at the smear on his fingers. 'Bastards!' he spat the word with venom. 'They'll hough the cattle by cutting their leg tendons to cripple them, if they can't get away.'

'Aye,' agreed Angus. 'But they're still near enough, and they don't know we're coming.' A wicked grin appeared on his face.

'Gather your men, JohnJoe, and see they're dealt with properly. Ackie MacBeth the bonesetter is with us. Keep a couple of the men and tell the rest to be quick after us. We'll meet you at Sandy's Corrie over the top of the pass, and we'll have those beasts for you.'

With that, he turned to his men. 'Well …' he paused for effect. 'What are we waiting for?'

As the others mounted, Ian Og hesitantly pointed to JohnJoe's shortsword and asked him, 'Can I? I'll see you get it back.'

'Here you are, laddie. God's blessing on it.'

The last of the words were spoken to Ian Og's back as he scrambled to sit up behind Dadda. Alistair was already gone after the raiders. Following them was easy enough. The turf was torn up and trampled along the route. Recently splintered small trees and branches clearly marked their progress. As JohnJoe surmised, the cattle were being driven east, at right angles to the pass. Alistair rode at breakneck speed across the rough ground, and was soon close enough to see the cattle ahead. Angus and the others were not far behind.

The herd was no longer being driven so hard and there was no sign of a rearguard, but it wouldn't do to be spotted. Alistair and Angus took stock. Obviously the thieves felt they were far enough away, and safe from pursuit by the drovers they had injured so badly. They had no idea that they were now the quarry of Alistair Glic and his men.

Following the trail slowly for another few minutes, Ian Og heard a quiet but triumphant 'Yess!' from Alistair. Not only had the herd slowed, it was turning south. The sweating horses were halted again. Dadda and Ian Og dismounted. The plan was for them to follow the trail directly, while the other two rode off to one side, where there was enough cover to pass unseen beyond the raiders.

The Corrieyairack hill was on their left. At the top of this glen there was shelter and a lochan, where stolen animals could rest up without being noticed. Alistair, Angus and Dadda had all run cattle in their time, and knew it well. They also knew that further up the advantage would be with the defenders. Down here where there was more cover and with surprise on their side, there was a very good chance of retrieving the herd before the enemy realised what was happening. Speed was vital.

Loping quietly in Dadda's footsteps, Ian Og was ignorant of all this. All he knew was that he was about to face a band of desperate thieves. Doubt wafted over him like an autumn mist and nervous sweat formed on his skin.

JohnJoe's sword was heavy and shorter than his father's, but it gave him courage and he slashed a couple of times at the air in front of him. As he strained to control its weight, his heartbeat pounded in his ears, and it was hard to say whether it was excitement or fear. He took another couple of swipes at the air.

'Time enough for that,' Dadda whispered, 'C'mon. This should do us. We have to find cover beside the track. It's our job to pick off these cattle thieves, and hope the cattle don't spread themselves across the whole countryside, or we'll be at this all day.'

His matter-of-fact tone checked the pounding in Ian Og's ears and chest. It told him that this was a job of work, which needed to be completed as swiftly and painlessly as possible. He took a deep breath and tried to look as calm as Dadda, while they stationed themselves several yards apart behind big boulders.

In the shadow of the rock, each detail of Ian Og's surroundings became sharply etched on his vision, greeny-grey crotal stuck to the stone; sharp brown fissures in the bark of a birch tree; a shiny black beetle with a pointed head making its way through the grass under the blue summer sky. When the sound of yelling and shouting rolled down the glen only a few minutes later, it startled him like a clap of thunder. The rumble of running cattle followed. He was about to crane his neck and look out towards them, but an angry shout from Dadda saved him from certain injury as the frightened cattle stampeded past his boulder.

Then it was quiet again. Ian Og peeped round the rock and was nearly beheaded by a large and very angry raider wielding a broadsword. Fortunately, instinct caused him to jerk up his own weapon in defence and blind fright gave him the strength to fight back. He had eyes only for the other's sword. It slashed left and right, low then high. Somehow he parried each thrust, nimbly moving leg or arm just in time, ducking and swerving as it missed him by inches. He was oblivious to everything but that murderous blade. Then his heel caught on a root. He fell backwards awkwardly as the attacker lurched forward. At the same time his arm came up.

Time stood still as he watched the tip of his sword penetrate the man's plaid and flesh, resisting at first and then yielding gently. There was no great surge of blood and an image of raw tripe rose in his mind, banished immediately as the man suddenly slumped forward. Ian Og was still in danger. It galvanised him. Yanking at his sword to free it, he rolled over quickly and scrambled to stand up. The raider collapsed onto the ground with a long quiet groan. Breathing in gulps, Ian Og stood over him, sword poised, waiting for the dead man to move.

It was a few moments before he was brought back to himself by a barrage of intense, angry, almost incoherent words. Turning he saw Alistair and Angus walking in the wake of the cattle and cursing with a coarse fluency that included Gaelic, Scots, French and several other languages.

'Damn it anyway, Angus!' Alistair covered a bloodied flap of skin on his arm, and was complaining in a loud voice. 'If you had just stayed where you were instead of trying to catch up with yon wee rat ...'

'Oh. So it's my fault that you weren't paying attention to the two men attacking you?'

'I was, but I was also paying attention to those three men you let slip past you. And the one you did get in the end nearly had you. You were beginning to need my assistance.'

'When did I ever need your assistance? Wee shite.'

'Many's the time old man, you always needed my assistance to cover up your mistakes.'

Despite the words, the bickering was good-natured and might have continued but Dadda stopped them. 'How bad is it?' he asked.

'I've had worse.'

'Give us a look,' said Dadda. He lifted Alistair's hand slightly from the wound. 'Yeuch! Ackie will stitch that, no bother. We'll try Grannie Morag's trick in the meantime.' He turned to Ian Og. 'Find me some sally rods. Nice long new ones. There'll be some by the water, I expect.'

The lad soon returned with a half a dozen green switches, and found the other three engulfed in a cloud of pipe smoke, gazing at Dadda's victim.

'So who were they?' said Angus, bending to check the man's sporran and taking the tobacco he found there. 'I don't recognise any of them. It's probably a MacGregor.'

Dadda nodded. 'Probably.'

He took the bunch of rods and gave them a twist before proceeding to pull down long thin strips from one of them. 'Do me a few more like this' he said to Ian Og and wound the willow thread around Alistair's wound. Within minutes the flesh was secure and the flow of blood was reduced to a trickle.

'Good old Grannie Morag,' Alistair said. 'Thanks,

Dadda. This'll do till we find Ackie.'

'And my Ian Og did very well' said Dadda proudly, nodding his head at the other dead raider. Pointedly he turned to Alistair. 'And he managed not to slice his arm off either when he took care of his man.'

'Yes, he did well,' Alistair sighed. 'But I think your lad is looking a bit pale now.' He raised his voice. 'Are you okay Ian Og? Let's take a look at your quarry.'

'The lad's very quiet,' said Dadda.

Ian Og was indeed feeling more than a bit queasy now that the rush of excitement had left him. He'd never killed a man before. Alistair indicated towards the dead man. 'Check yours, Ian Og. There might be something useful in his sporran, and take that sword.'

Reluctantly, Ian Og turned his assailant over. He gasped, before turning aside and puking up the day's food. It was MacCannie, his captor near Fort William. Alistair couldn't believe it. Ian Og had slain MacCannie.

'Take the sword, laddie,' said Angus. 'It's rightly yours now.'

But Ian Og shook his head. 'I want nothing of that vile man. It's tainted.' And he turned and got sick again.

'It'll do for someone else in time, so we'll take it anyway,' said Dadda. 'There's some siller in his sporran. We'll take that too. There's little enough in the glen.'

Then he nodded to Alistair and Angus. 'You two mount up and go on ahead. We'll take our time and gather up the few stray animals on our way.'

Further along the glen, the highlanders, with plaids flapping, arms waving and loud yells, managed to turn the cantering beasts towards the main track and the pass. Although there was more room to spread out, the animals were tiring fast, and without being harassed into further exertions, soon slowed to a walk and began to graze the grass at their feet. Alistair and Angus organised the men to gather them up, and by the time Ian Og and Dadda got there, the animals were quiet and Alistair finally submitted his arm to Ackie MacBeth's needle and horsehair. JohnJoe with the help of his defeated men soon joined them.

There were two badly injured animals. Loud bellowing drew Dadda and Ian Og to a beast with a broken leg. He lay on the bracken watching the men approach, his head weaving back and forward, and keeping up a mournful distress call.

'You must be hungry,' said Dadda.

'Oh yes,' sighed an exhausted Ian Og.

'Have you meal in your sporran?'

'I have. Mamma gave it to me before we left.'

'Put a dollop into your horn'.

They approached the distressed animal. Five of the men gathered were there holding out horns. Those with oat or barley meal had already crumbed grain into theirs. Dadda knelt down, and ignoring the jerking of the animal, he lifted her head firmly and made an incision in her neck with his knife. Blood bubbled into each cup that was passed down to him.

Those who arrived too late crossed over to where the other stricken animal lay, still bellowing its pain, and again Dadda put it out of its misery as soon as all had supped its bounty.

Within an hour, the cattle were quiet as if nothing untoward had occurred in their day. The last of the strays were gathered in. The two dead animals were skinned while warm, and the quarters tied to several horses. When the herd was calm enough to be moved along the track, only the lower gut was left for the buzzards. The rest was carried by horse or man, with even the offal knotted safely in plaid ends.

Once the herd had been recovered, there was little chance to sleep, because they had to keep a constant watch against retaliation. Fortunately, two of JohnJoe's men had suffered nothing worse than a sore head. It meant the MacDonells did not have to stay with the cattle for very long, but they were still honour-bound to see the drove safely on its way south.

It was the drover with the broken leg who had caused the worst problem. He could not be left on his own. The raiders would be watching and would set upon him, even if he had an escort, so he was hoisted onto Pepper's back and had gone with Angus. Ackie MacBeth had set his leg between two splints of wood, and by the time they reached Dalwhinnie he was able to hobble with a crutch under each arm. Angus had taken pity on him and agreed to take him by an alternative route to his family, near Aberchalder at the head of Loch Oich. There he would be safe to recover.

CHAPTER 17

I̲t̲ ̲w̲a̲s̲ ̲a̲n̲ ̲a̲n̲x̲i̲o̲u̲s̲ ̲H̲a̲m̲i̲s̲h̲ who was first to spot a weary Alistair on his horse approaching the croft, followed by Dadda, Uncle Roderick and Ian Og. The grain was sprouting, and although he had turned it carefully every day, he would be reassured to know he was doing the job properly, but his heart sank. He could see they had been in a fight, and Angus wasn't with them.

It was nearly Mamma's time but seeing the straggle coming up the track, she waddled out to greet them. She hugged Dadda to make sure he was all in one piece. Grannie Morag, being ever practical, put broth on the fire to warm, and filled a large jug with ale and another with whisky, and set them on the table. When the men drew close enough for her to inspect them properly, she turned to Hamish. 'Go and tell Alistair not to worry about the horse. You'll see to it.' Then she said to Sarah, who was standing in the doorway, 'Fetch me some of the dried meadowsweet. I think we'll need it.'

By the loud chatter and teasing between the travellers and the children who came to welcome them home, it might not have been immediately obvious that the men, bowing their heads when they entered the croft, were exceedingly tired. Dark rings circled bloodshot eyes, and Alistair in particular looked very frail and shaken. With sighs of relief the men sat and took the whisky and ale offered. They teased the youngsters who brought them food, and who listened wide-eyed while they related their adventures.

'So Angus is in Aberchalder?' said a relieved Hamish, when he heard the story. 'Is it very far?'

'No, it's not that far,' said Dadda. 'Why? Are you worried he'll get lost?'

'No. I just wondered. How long would it take him, two or three days?'

'Och, aye.' Dadda didn't really answer the question, but sounded very confident that his brother-in-law would arrive soon.

There was plenty of talk from the youngsters who stayed at home, about what was going on while Dadda and Roderick were away. Uncle Ranald and Hamish spent much of the fine weather out at the peat bank, cutting sods for the winter fires. The children were not exempt from this work either. Eileen explained proudly to her Dadda that everyone had a job this year, except Mamma because she couldn't bend down.

Everyone laughed at her serious description of the family's hard work, cutting and saving the peat. Alistair listened as he sat, white-faced and quiet, with his head resting against the wall and a fixed smile on his face. Hamish judged it might be the right time to ask him some of the questions that were bothering him.

'Alistair,' he asked, trying to sound casual. 'You and Angus used to do all sorts of things together, didn't you?'

'Yes. I suppose we did. He was like my big brother sometimes, rather than an uncle.'

'Em ... Did you ever make whisky with him? I thought he would be back by now.'

'He should get here tomorrow, I expect, or the next day maybe. So how long has it been?'

'Four days.'

'Only four days?' Alistair shook his head slowly. 'It seems longer.' Then he remembered the matter in hand. 'And you've been turning it every day?'

'Aye, I have. What if he doesn't get back by the time it's sprouted?'

'I'm sure he will be. It's only Aberchalder. But I expect he'll be pleased if you and Ian Og get the kiln ready and gather in some good dry peat.'

'Thanks, Alistair. I might do some of that today.' Hamish was much happier now. Just talking about his worries cheered him greatly. The kiln area was already cleared, but he was cautious about doing more, in case it might not be right. However, with Ian Og's help, he realised, it should all be okay.

Alistair laid his head back against the wall again. He was very quiet. He took another large pull at the whisky, but it didn't seem to warm him at all. Grannie Morag came over and put a hand to his forehead. She had watched him carefully since she first spotted the pale face riding slowly towards the croft. Now, with a hand to his forehead, she said, 'You've got a fever. I'll make up a little toddy with the meadowsweet.' With eyes closed, Alistair grimaced at the thought.

'And don't look like that, boy,' Grannie's smile belied

her words. 'I can still give any of these lads a good clip on the ear, and you're no bigger than some of them.' She began to peel back the cloth on his arm. 'I'd better take a look at this, while I'm about it.' Her inspection was as one professional assessing another's work.

Ian Og leaned forward to take a look at the injury. He drew his head back swiftly and wrinkled his nose. 'Pooh!'

'Aye,' said Grannie Morag. 'It's neat enough, but it smells bad and it's still very soggy. We'll try soaking it in salt water. That should help, Sarah! Bring me that bucket of water and put salt into it.'

By now, the children were drifting away. The chatter of the tired men was petering out, and Grannie Morag's summons to Sarah was the signal for the rest to scatter. Ian Og went with Hamish to see the sprouting grain. Dadda and Roderick said they should go and help Ranald attend to some of the heavy work before they turned in. They excused themselves, leaving Alistair waiting for the ministrations of the women.

Grannie Morag sent Mamma off to rest, and told Sarah to make up a bed space for Alistair, while she prepared another hot draught of meadowsweet and honey toddy. It tasted very strange, but under her stern gaze Alistair managed to drink it all. Soon, he broke out in a sweat. Tiredness gradually overwhelmed him and he passed out. The two women didn't take long to strip and settle him onto the bed of springy bracken near the fire. With a calf hide under him and plaid to cover him, he slept for many hours.

When he opened his eyes it was dark, and he couldn't remember where he was. There was a faint red glimmer from the fire. The rest was a fog. A malevolent weight seemed to lie on his shoulder, and a great lethargy prevented him from moving. He was thirsty. As he smacked his lips to try and make some spittle, he felt his head being gently lifted and a horn cup put to his mouth.

There was the strong taste of meadowsweet and honey again, but it was cool. He slurped noisily as he tried to rinse it around his mouth. The next time he tried to focus his eyes it was daylight and he was given another drink. 'Thank you,' he murmured as sleep overtook him again.

When the household rose in the morning, Grannie came to check on the patient and found Sarah dozing beside him.

'His colour is terrible still,' said Grannie.

'What about the arm, Grannie Morag?' asked Sarah 'I washed it in salt several times, but it looks awful.'

The older woman nodded. 'It's not healing right. I'll get my knife. We have to get the poison out.' She turned to young Morag who was watching. 'Go and ask Uncle Ranald if he can come and help me.'

Grandmother and granddaughter began to busy themselves, getting cloths and bowls ready to mop up whatever poison they could extract. Many a boil was lanced with the same paraphernalia, and it was never a pretty sight.

Grannie Morag's special knife for surgery was long and thin. It was ground and honed to whisper sharpness, and on a strip of fine leather she now gave it several strokes, to strop the edge to complete perfection. Having plucked a single hair from her own head and sliced it along its length, she nodded. 'It'll do. Right, Ranald. Come and hold him steady for me. It shouldn't bother him too much but we'd best be careful. Sarah, you give him that whisky and then hold his head and talk gently to him. We should be done, almost before he feels it.'

Grannie lifted her voice to rouse the sleeping man. Awake he was more likely to co-operate with her work. Asleep, his response would be uncertain.

'Alistair, take a good pull of the whisky,' she said with authority. His eyelids reluctantly unglued themselves and he looked out in a daze. As he drank the half-cup of whisky, she said, 'This won't take long.'

'Mmm....,' he replied sleepily, as his eyes slowly blinked shut.

She nodded to her assistants. Ranald was kneeling on the other side of the recumbent invalid, firmly gripping wrist, upper arm and elbows rigid, to counter any sudden body movement. Sarah cradled Alistair's head and began to speak quietly.

'Grannie's very good at this, Alistair. I think she gets the angels to help her.' She watched as the older woman crossed herself before confidently taking the knife in hand. The soft words continued. 'You'll soon have a girl in your arms again.'

There was a little pause as Sarah thought about this. 'I suppose you have a girl. What kind of girl do you like? I wonder. I don't suppose she's like me. Is she one of the town girls, maybe? Pretty, I expect. Or maybe she is a cousin. Perhaps I know her. I don't suppose I'd like her.' The words flowed quietly over the still form as Grannie Morag began her work.

A very swift touch of the knife along the length of Ackie MacBeth's stitch work was all that was required to unleash evil-smelling black and yellow pus from the newly gaping wound. Quickly, salt water was drenched over the flesh to rinse off the last of the poison. Alistair jerked. Sarah held him firm and tried to reassure him as one would a child. 'There, there. It'll soon be all over. There, there. You'll soon be with your girl again; you'll be smiling at her with those sparkling eyes and white teeth ...'

The work was almost over, and the old lady was relieved to see red blood flowing from the wound, as she closed the flesh firmly together, and restitched it with fine linen thread. On top she laid a poultice of mashed dead nettles and willow bark, and the whole area was bandaged with long linen strips. 'That should hold him. Thank you, Ranald.' Turning to her granddaughter, she said, 'Sarah, we'll need more nettles, but first we'd better get rid of all this mess.'

It was two more days before Alistair truly woke up. He felt weak. His arm still felt bruised and sore, but it was not the pulsating swollen mass it had been. Once again a gentle hand lifted his head to give him a drink, and for the first time he looked at his benefactor. Sarah smiled down at him.

'God, Sarah,' he complained. 'That stuff is terrible.'

'But it seems to be doing you good,' she replied. 'And Grannie Morag said you had to drink every drop.'

'Ah go on,' he wheedled. 'I could really use a mug of ale. My mouth is very dry.'

She looked down at him. 'Well ...'

'Ah go on. Just give me a mug of cool ale, or a dish of tea. I know she likes tea, your Grannie.'

It wasn't easy to resist Alistair Glic when he piled on the charm, and Sarah didn't try. She laughed and brought a large bowl of ale. As he gulped it, she added, 'And Grannie says you can have some broth too.'

'I'm not sure I can face it.'

The smell of hot chicken broth however, made

specially by Grannie Morag, plump with barley and laced with all manner of wild herbs, would have brought Lazarus from his cold tomb. Although he was weak, Alistair was not near death's door, and suddenly realised he was very hungry indeed. Despite the ache in his arm he would have taken spoon and bowl and helped himself, except it was very pleasant being gently fed by Sarah. With each spoonful, she smiled encouragingly as she would for the children, and he thought to himself how comely she was.

Her mop of dark hair with its untidy plaits fringed a pleasant face, and when the food was carried towards his mouth, her own mouth opened encouragingly and then closed with a smile, as his lips engulfed the warm broth.

When they saw he was awake, the twins Eileen and Morag came to have a look at Alistair, but somewhat disappointingly he fell sound asleep as soon as he'd swallowed the last mouthful of broth. Sarah stood up and shooed them away as Grannie Morag came to check on her patient.

'Aye, he'll do,' she said, noting the improved pink colour in his face. 'And it's time you got some rest too, miss. You've had little sleep yourself over the past two days.'

'I'm all right, Grannie Morag.'

'Nonsense,' she said firmly. 'Look at him. See, he's fine now. He'll be a bit stiff for a day or two but he will be right as rain. Off you go and get some rest.'

CHAPTER 18

Hᴀᴍɪsʜ ᴀɴᴅ Iᴀɴ Oɢ ᴡᴇʀᴇ relieved when Alistair was eventually back on his feet. It had been seven days and there was still no sign of Angus. All the grain was sprouted, and the next day it was due to go into the kiln. Over the past few days they neglected the animals to spend every spare minute up at the hideout, trying to remember how it was all supposed to be arranged.

Built between two great boulders, it had a circular chimney, with a loose lattice of sticks forming a floor halfway up. Bracken would be laid on this and then some coarse cloth to let smoke from the fire below rise through it, while preventing the grain falling down.

When Angus had finished his previous batch, he left the walls almost intact, but disguised them with sods and piles of stones. With the help of Wee Anghie, Ian Og and Hamish pulled most of these out of the way, in order to clear out the flue hole at the bottom, and make sure there would be a good draught when the fire was lit. They also replaced a couple of the sticks that looked a bit fragile. Only a covering of bracken on the completed lattice would be needed when they returned.

That evening, Alistair sat near the fire taking notice of everything going on in the room. Although he was still a little weak, he was reverting to his former cheerful self, teasing Mamma about when they were young and she was put in charge of him.

'Aye, and you and Angus would run away on me, and I would be left having to explain how I lost you.'

'We'd be up in the glen, swinging on trees or making a dam at the waterfall, so that we could swim under it.' He winked at the little ones.

'Lucky you didn't get killed.' Wee Morag was a pragmatist.

'He nearly did … by me!' Mamma laughed.

The children were becoming used to seeing their cousin Alistair asleep in the corner. When he was awake, they kept asking about when he was a child like them. Grannie Morag also told them funny stories of when Dadda, Uncle Roderick and Uncle Ranald were little.

As the day went on, the gathering in the darkened croft became a ceilidh, with stories and gossip, whisky and ale passing around the room. Uncle Roderick was persuaded to bring out his fiddle. He had made it himself in a square shape, and although he couldn't match James the Lion, he was able to make lively tunes for dancing, or he could accompany a song or two. When Wee Anghie played with him on his whistle, the music echoed from the house down through the glen. Even gentle Uncle Ranald could 'deedle deedle' well enough for dancing and was a popular visitor in crofts where there were young people wanting to ceilidh.

Everyone was drawn into it and applauded for their efforts. Apart from knowing all the choruses, each of the little ones showed their party pieces, songs, rhymes and recitations. The party was warm and friendly. Yet again, Grannie Morag told her story of the battle of Locheil in which the MacDonells routed the Camerons, and there were cheers at every thrust of a sword or dagger into some dastardly opponent's gizzard. No matter how many times Grannie retold those events, people still wanted to hear her version again and again.

When it was Sarah's turn she gazed into the fire, and sang a song that Mamma taught her many years before.

I will wear my hair beneath my shawl
Because my lad has gone away
The wind whispers into my ear
I can hear him across the sea

Her voice was clear and pleasant, and carried the simple little song tunefully. Alistair was moved. He had never heard such haunting sadness in the song before. Dadda was cheerfully proud of his daughter. 'What do you think of that? Isn't she a great girl? My wee Sarah! Come here and give your old Dadda a kiss.'

Then it was time for Ian Og's story of the water horse. A chorus of voices joined him in the opening words: 'Once there was a prince who lived under the water in Loch Ness.' It was a tale of impossible love between the prince and a beautiful maiden. It ended with: 'If you walk along the side of Loch Ness, you can still hear the splashing of the water horses, and if you look carefully you may see three young ones playing together.' Then everybody chorused the last few words together: 'Kenneth, Donald and Seanna'.

Grannie Morag and Sarah sighed together, each pondering the difficult course of true love.

Mamma looked down at the young ones who were trying hard to stay awake. 'It's time for bed.'

It was a signal for the ceilidh to end. Everyone began to move, and head towards their bed space or corner.

The following morning, Hamish was anxiously asking Dadda and Uncle Roderick the same thing he'd asked every day that week: 'Do you think Uncle Angus will get here today?' It bothered him that that neither Ian Og nor any of the men of the family were very concerned that the journey to Aberchalder was taking longer than estimated. For them there was no doubt that Angus was well able to take care of himself. He could be affable and charming, but was also skilled with sword and musket when the need arose. Besides, he was known and welcome in many a croft, and bad news would reach them more swiftly than a plague.

Hamish's real problem was that an anxious Lizzie had expected him home several days ago. Having been responsible for the sprouting of the grain, he didn't want to leave the job half-finished.

When by mid morning there was still no sign of man or horse, Hamish sought out Alistair, who was supposed to be helping Sarah bring in some stray sheep. Really he was just keeping her company, as she and the dog rounded up the animals and headed them towards the croft. When Hamish found them, Sarah was laughing and Alistair had a big silly grin on his face.

'Ah Hamish, I was just telling Sarah she'd better mind that dog or the sheep will be halfway across the mountains in minutes.'

The anxious young man was not interested in ragged sheep, and got to the point straight away. 'It's eight days. I think the grain should be going into the kiln.'

Alistair understood. 'Yes. I suppose so. It must be quite important if Angus can't get back in time.' He thought for a moment. 'I'll give you a hand if you like and we'll get Ian Og as well.' He turned graciously and bowed. 'That is, if Sarah can do without my assistance and advice.'

'What advice and assistance?' Sarah said rather too heartily. 'I only let you come because I was sorry for you.' Turning to Hamish, she said, 'Take him. He's just been keeping me back with all his stories.'

Sarah was telling herself that Alistair's presence was distracting her from getting up to the little nooks and corners of the hill, where stray sheep were often to be found. She didn't want to consider how he disturbed her in other ways.

Hamish pressed home his opportunity. 'Well, Ian Og is very good, but I would be grateful if you could take a look. I don't want to set your arm off again.' Hamish was caught between not wanting to relinquish his kingdom, and needing to get the job done right.

Alistair sensed that Sarah would be more comfortable if he helped Hamish. 'I don't think checking some grain will do that,' he said, trying to hide his disappointment. 'And it'll have to be today because I've been away too long. I'll need to get back. The chief will be expecting me.'

Sarah stood silent and slowly took a deep breath. Alistair no longer needed her. It was a wrench, but at the same time it felt like a weight had been taken off her shoulders. She stood up straight and smiled determinedly. 'Thanks, Alistair,' she said and waited expectantly.

'Will we go now?' Alistair asked Hamish.

'I think we ought to get up there as soon as we can,' said Hamish. 'We'll collect Ian Og on the way.'

As Sarah watched them go, a lump like a stone stuck in her throat. If she could have re-enacted the past couple of minutes, she would have tried not to be so foolish. Alistair must think her a very silly child. She sighed deeply and thought of the smile that crinkled up the corner of his eyes, and made her heart beat a little faster. Without him life would be less exciting. Perhaps this feeling was only because she had been watching over him for four days and nights, and maybe she was still very tired.

Sarah would have been surprised if she knew that, for Alistair, the persistent image in his mind was of a girl with greenish-hazel eyes, dark eyebrows and a mop of curly black hair and untidy plaits. He'd told Hamish he was needed at Keppoch, but the people there already knew the herd was safe, and the chief was by now in Edinburgh. It was Sarah's offhand dismissal that had made him feel he should be moving on.

Clearly she found life uncomfortable when he was around, so he mustn't rip the new stitches in his arm, because Grannie Morag would insist on him remaining while the wound healed, and Sarah would be forced to look after him. Without realising it, his face softened and he smiled at the thought. However, he realised it would be sweet torture to stay any longer.

Hamish and Ian Og had already arranged a loose turf sod thatch at the top of the kiln chimney, to keep the rain out and let smoke through. The sprouted grain lay on the upper level. They checked everything but they were not sure if they should go ahead.

'Shall we light the fire now?' Ian Og asked when the three were together. 'What do you think Alistair?'

'I'm not sure … it looks right.' Alistair pondered the problem. 'It would need an eye kept on it. If we light it now we will have to stay here all night. Probably better tomorrow when we've all had some rest. I think we should go back to the croft now. It's getting late.'

'Aye,' agreed Ian Og. 'I think Grannie Morag will want to make sure your arm is still working.'

'It's fine now. A bit tired but it feels good.'

'Right,' Ian Og said purposefully. 'I'll come up early tomorrow and get it lit, and you two can be heading home. Hamish will have to face his mother, but he can truly say how much we needed him.'

This having been decided, they blocked the flue hole of the kiln with stones and earth to discourage pilfering rodents, and returned to the croft where hot broth and the family were waiting for them.

'I'll be glad when Angus gets back home,' said Mamma to Ian Og. 'And I've hardly seen you since you came back from Auntie Kate's.'

'The boy's doing well. They all are,' Dadda said, trying to lighten the mood.

'We couldn't leave Angus in the lurch' said Alistair nudging his two helpers. 'We men must stick together, Mary.'

'Men you say! Hmph,' was Grannie Morag's opinion. 'You're always killing yourselves and then expect us to patch you up. I must make sure you haven't sent your arm bad again.' There was a hint of dire warning within her remark, as she unwound the cloth and leaves from Alistair's arm. 'Hmm …' was the only sound she made as she inspected the wound. She made no other comment. Clearly, this was a good sign and there was a sigh of relief from all sitting around the fire.

'He's fine, Grannie,' said Ian Og, smiling.

'Yes.' There was a nod and the hint of pride in her work. 'But don't you go messing it up now, young Alistair.'

'Alistair and Hamish will be off in the morning,' said Ian Og. 'We'll go and get the kiln fired up first, and then it can wait till Uncle Angus gets back, so I'll be here to help you, Grannie.'

'Good,' Mamma said, sitting down rather heavily. 'Oh, dear,' she added, as she looked around at a damp patch on the chair. 'I think this is it, Grannie.'

'Aye' nodded the older woman. 'Let's get you to the other room.'

The rest of the company was quiet until the two women withdrew, and then the chatter broke out. 'Well, well,' said Dadda, taking the jug of whisky and pouring a good splash for each of the men. 'It won't be long now. She doesn't usually take long.'

Sarah frowned as she remembered the birth of Auntie Kate's wee baby at The Weaver's a few short weeks ago. It had been painful for Kate, and now it was Mamma's turn.

'Here, take a sup of this.' Dadda poured whisky into Sarah's bowl. 'Don't look so worried. If she gets them this far, your mother never has any trouble.'

'I hope so.' She hardly noticed the burning in her mouth, but felt a great burst of warmth in her stomach.

'Oh yes,' Dadda hid his concern under a confident tone. 'And with Grannie Morag it'll all be fine.'

After a while Grannie Morag returned to the room. 'I don't think it'll be for some time yet,' she said. 'You may as well get the children bedded down. I'll stay with her.'

'Do you want me to help, Grannie?' Sarah asked. 'Shall I come through?'

'You're a good girl, Sarah. Mamma and I have done this a few times. I expect we'll manage fine. Besides, we have Dadda to help us if we need it.' She looked down at her son who returned her gaze in panic, until he realised she was only teasing him.

'Wee Anghie and the twins can go in for a few minutes. She'll be glad of a little company to say her prayers. The men leave these things to us and God, you see.' She nudged Dadda as she said this, but continued talking to Sarah. 'Then you can keep her company for a while.'

When the children were settled down to sleep, Sarah went through into the small room. Mamma was lying in bed, her rosary beads still wrapped around her fingers. By the light of the candle, she looked a bit tired, but was not in any distress. 'Ah, Sarah, it's you. Come to see how your Mamma is doing?'

Sarah nodded, not sure what to say.

'Come and give me a hug. You know it'll be hard work for me, but it'll be worth it in the end. That's how I got you and I was much worse then.'

'Really, Mamma?' Sarah was curious. 'How do you mean?'

'It was awful. I didn't know what was going to happen. The midwife was an old woman from Bohuntin. Folk over there said she was great, and she came up to stay a couple of weeks before you were due. She always looked strange and talked funny, and she bossed everyone around. Then when the time came, she began to put all kinds of strange branches around the bed, and was praying very loud. I got very frightened and began to cry, but she wasn't very nice and told me to be quiet or the fairies would come and take my baby.'

'So what happened?'

'Obviously, the fairies came and gave me the wrong baby.'

Sarah found herself laughing. 'Mamma, what really happened?'

'Your Grannie Morag came in to see what all the noise was about, and saw that the woman was very drunk and threw her out.' Mamma clenched her teeth as the pain struck her, and then breathed heavily to try and ease it. When the spasm was over she continued. 'Grannie Morag gave me a big hug and a large glass of whisky with something in it to calm me down, and we didn't do such a bad job in the end, did we?'

'No,' said Sarah. 'I suppose not.'

Grannie Morag came in to check her charge. 'Hungry?' she asked Mamma.

'No. But I'll take a drink of water, something cool.'

'It's time to let your Mamma get some rest,' the old woman said when she returned. 'It'll be a long night.'

CHAPTER 19

As she closed the door behind her, Sarah was relieved to leave the two women to their work. In the main room the company was quiet. Anghie and the twins were settled into the corner where Alistair had lain, and although they were determined to stay awake for the birth of a new brother or sister, the twins were soon fast asleep. Wee Anghie was making a better stab at staying awake, but also lost the battle. Alistair and Ian Og were to bed down in the byre with the rest of the men.

Hamish was anxious to leave. 'I'd better be going home. There's nothing more for me to do here or at the kiln.'

The family stood to shake his hand and thank him for all his work while they were away. He gathered his bundle and they watched as he set off down the trail.

'D'ye know,' said Alistair to Ian Og, 'I reckon we'd probably be as well off up at the kiln. There'll be precious little sleep around this house tonight.'

'Can I come?' Sarah asked. 'Mamma doesn't need me and I don't think Dadda needs me either, so I'd rather come with you.'

This was a dilemma for them, because they were sworn not to show anyone where the kiln was, and already Hamish was working up there. Taking Sarah would be another breach, but the circumstances were very special, and not taking her when she needed their company would be a bit mean.

'So long as you don't tell anyone,' said Ian Og .

'I won't,' she promised, even though she already knew where it was.

'Ever,' said Ian Og. 'Cross your heart.'

'Cross my heart,' she agreed. In truth, they knew she would never tell.

'Good,' said Alistair. 'She'll help us shield the fire from any spies.'

'She's so fat you mean,' Ian Og said

Sarah protested. 'Alistair, you're rotten!'

Disconcerted that Sarah might have taken his words amiss, Alistair hurriedly explained through the laughter of the other two. 'What I meant was that it's another pair of hands to help us build up some cover, so the light doesn't spread all over the glen.' He hesitated and added, 'And when the work is done, I'll be on my way.'

'You can't just go like that,' Ian Og gave voice to Sarah's unspoken thoughts.

'I've already told everyone I'm going tomorrow,' said Alistair. 'They'll all be too busy to notice whether I'm here or not.' What he really wanted to say was that he knew Sarah would be too busy to notice his absence. 'So when we've finished up at the kiln, I'll head off. I'm just another mouth to feed and get in the way. Hamish has already gone.'

There was such finality in his words that Sarah didn't protest. 'Well, you'd better say goodbye to Dadda and the uncles now.'

The farewell took more time than anticipated, because Dadda insisted that they should toast the departing guest with a large *deoch an dorus* (drink for the door), and was only prevented from setting another round by Uncle Ranald dutifully pointing out that Grannie Morag said they should all get some rest.

By the time Alistair drained the last drop, Sarah was gathering bannocks into a cloth to bring up the hill, before making sure that the children were safely asleep in the corner of the room. Ian Og took some of the resinous pine twigs which were kept beside the hearth and stuck them into his sporran.

Outside there was another delay because Alistair's horse was nervous, and wouldn't come to halter, but eventually Sarah was sitting in the saddle and Ian Og on its rump. Although it was late, there was still enough light in the fine summer sky to climb up to Angus's hideout. In order to confuse anyone watching or trailing them, Alistair led the horse and its passengers into some birch trees, before checking the area.

At the hideout he could see that Hamish and Ian Og had been busy. Plenty of dry peat was stacked alongside the kiln, covered by an old cowhide to keep rain off. The piled stones were already cleared from the flue, and stacked to form a shield against prying eyes, but without impeding the flow of air. Alistair beckoned the others to join him.

It took only a moment or two to kindle a spark with flint and tinder, and nurse it with dry grass and bracken. Ian Og added a couple of the resinous sticks, which took light with a satisfying burst. Then the peat was carefully set on top so it wouldn't throttle the new life out of the fire.

At first, the fumes rose in a cloud. It got into their

eyes and made them cough, but Angus's spot was well chosen. The natural draught between the rocks in the dish-shaped clearing began to draw the smoke up through the chimney, once the fire was established.

They stood watching the glow. 'Do you think we can be seen?' asked Alistair.

'No, I don't think so.' Ian Og tried to assess the work. 'We built up the stones quite a lot. You'd have to get up really close to see us, and the peat fire doesn't roar and spark like the wood fires.'

To make sure, Sarah built up the stone shield even higher, and the other two nodded their approval. The kiln was as protected as it could be, and there was little to do now. The fire must be tended and the grain turned from time to time, until it was baked and ready for grinding, a job that could wait for Angus's return.

They were all hungry now. Sarah brought out the bannocks.

'It's been a busy few weeks,' Alistair mused.

'It certainly had its moments,' said Sarah. 'You must have thought I was awfully bad-tempered when I shouted at you, that day you brought Ian Og back from Corran.'

'No, no,' Alistair lied. 'You were worried about Kate.'

'I was,' Sarah nodded. 'I was frightened.'

'I'd never have guessed it,' Alistair said admiringly.

'It'll be quiet again when you've gone,' Ian Og was wistful.

'Yes,' said Sarah.

'Will you miss me?'

Sarah sensed that this was addressed to her, but Ian Og answered, 'Oh yes. I want to know more about all of those places you've been to.'

'Perhaps Sarah will be able to tell you all about them when I write to her.'

'Write to her? She can't read!' Ian Og scoffed.

'Well, she's been learning with Hamish and maybe you'll help her too.'

'She's a girl!' Ian Og was scornful, which drew his sister's ire.

'Lots of girls can read.'

'Mamma can't,' Ian Og presented what he thought would be an unanswerable argument.

'Grannie Morag can,' Sarah countered.

'Well, Grannie Morag can do anything,' Alistair said, trying to placate them both. 'And I'm sure Ian Og will be happy to help you with your reading and writing, because I told you before, I want to get letters from you.'

'That would be good,' Sarah agreed, looking at her brother.

'I don't see why I should,' said Ian Og, pouting. He would be a reluctant teacher.

'You'll do it for me,' Alistair said, adding, 'because I'm asking you.'

'Whisht!' said Sarah, alarmed at a sudden noise. The others heard it too. Someone or something was heading towards them on horseback. All three jumped up.

'Oh God, don't let it be the gaugers,' whispered Ian Og.

'Here! Smother the fire a bit,' Alistair said, quickly drawing ashes over it, making it darker within the little clearing. Quickly they withdrew into cover. Sarah ducked into a clump of bushes while Alistair and Ian Og threw themselves full length on the ground under bracken fronds, where they could observe anyone approaching, and crawl away quietly if it turned out to be excise men.

Slowly but steadily, the hooves approached along the side of the hill. Finally the little horse stepped into the clearing and halted.

'It's Pepper!' Ian Og gaped in astonishment at the riderless animal.

'Where's Angus?' Sarah whispered back. 'Something must have happened to him.'

'I'm right behind you, my pet,' said a familiar voice.

Sarah nearly jumped out of her skin, and only just managed to stop herself from letting out a screech. 'Uncle Angus!' she said in her loudest and most indignant whisper. 'You scared me to death!'

The other two crawled out from under cover.

'Alistair and Ian Og, what are you all doing here?' Angus kept his voice low.

'We're baking the grain,' Ian Og said. 'We thought you were never getting back.'

'Fair play to you, boy,' said Angus, smiling.

Suddenly there was another sound. Someone else was approaching. Alistair, Sarah and Ian Og automatically ducked, until they heard Hamish's voice. 'All safe, Angus?' he said.

'Yes, all safe, Ruach.'

'Hamish!' Sarah was surprised. 'I thought you were heading home.'

'I was, but when I met Angus at the bottom of the glen, he knew I wanted to see the work finished so he changed my mind.'

Soon they were all sitting around the kiln fire, staring into the embers and finishing off the bannocks. Angus stood up and went outside. After a few minutes he returned with a corked earthenware jug that still bore soil from its hiding place.

After taking a good mouthful, he passed it to

Alistair. Hamish brought out his horn to be filled. The jug then passed to Sarah who took a big gulp and was grateful. She wouldn't have thought to let Ian Og have any, but when he held out his hand, she changed her mind. He'd worked hard enough for his share. As he coughed on the spirits, Angus retrieved the jug, saying, 'That's enough, laddie. Your Mamma will kill me.'

It was Ian Og who asked the question everyone wanted answered. 'So, Uncle Angus, what kept you so long? We were all worried.'

There was plenty of news to tell his audience. After the MacDonells had left the herd, Angus, as agreed, took the injured drover to his family. They had one encounter with raiders on the way, out to rob them of Pepper and any food they might have. The injured drover used his crutches to good effect, beating any who came near him and the pony, while Angus dealt with the rest. Once out of the mountains, they faced no more danger, and made good time to Aberchalder.

Word of the attack had already reached the man's family, and the welcome for Angus and his injured friend was heartfelt. They insisted the Good Samaritan should rest for a while and join them to celebrate MacCannie's death. There was talk that three of MacCannie's sons were with him that day. Their notoriety had already begun to overtake their father's. Cattle were the least of it. Whole villages suffered their infamy and no one was safe. Knowing this and seeing their own drover safely home was a great relief to them.

The neighbours then arrived to celebrate the drover's return. A ceilidh soon developed and Angus thought it would have been rude to leave when they were treating him like a hero. So it was next day when he had to tell them that there was grain malting, and he had to get back, or all would be lost.

As Angus was talking, Alistair prepared himself to leave. Angus examined his injured arm and was happy to see that Grannie had made a good job of stitching it all together, and he was well enough to be on his way home.

'Your whisky was a big help,' Sarah assured her uncle. 'And now it'll be helping Mamma with the baby.'

'That's happening now?' said Angus, arching an eyebrow.

'Yes. That's one of the reasons we made ourselves scarce.'

He looked down at Sarah. 'I thought you'd be the expert. What with Kate and all you did?'

'Oh no!' she protested. 'I am no expert. It's worse than when the cows calve. I'm really glad Grannie Morag is there.'

Angus laughed. 'I suppose she has the most experience.'

As dawn broke, the five of them were still at the kiln. Ian Og was leaning back against the shelter of piled stones, his responsibility at an end, dozing in and out of sleep. Angus tended the fire while Sarah also dozed, watched over by Alistair and Hamish, who were still discussing the raid and its aftermath.

Eventually, Angus said, 'It'll do. Let's get down to the croft and see how they're doing. We'll get the grain stored away later.'

'I'll be off then,' said Hamish, rising.

'Are you going now?' Sarah asked, rubbing sleep out of her eyes.

'Yes. I met my cousin Lachie who will tell my folk that I was going with Angus, but I had better show my face, or my Mammy will think something terrible has happened to me again.'

'If she knows you're with Angus Sticks, she will know that something terrible has probably happened to you,' Alistair said.

'Cheeky pup!' said Angus, taking it all in good part.

Sarah was a little awkward now that Alistair was finally taking his leave. She wanted it to last a bit longer. 'I'll come and help you with the horse, in case it's loose or anything.'

'That's kind,' Alistair smiled at her.

If Hamish noticed anything meaningful in the exchange, he gave no sign, and the three of them walked out together to fetch the horse. Angus and Ian Og tidied up around the kiln, scattering the remains of the fire. The wind would remove all the fine ash and they would camouflage the site later in the day.

As Hamish walked ahead, Alistair mounted his horse. Sarah looked up at him. 'I hope your arm is as good as new now.'

'It nearly is,' he said, and, taking her chin in his hand, tilted it up and kissed her gently on the forehead once again. 'Thank you.' He settled himself in the saddle and quietly added, 'And I've no other girl to dance with.'

He tapped the horse's side with his heels, and went ahead to pick up Hamish. He was gone before Sarah realised what he had said.

As Sarah, Ian Og and Angus came down the hill, the croft lay before them. In the early summer morning light it looked peaceful, nestling for shelter against a small rise. Grass and weeds in the sod thatch, turned it freshly green and colourful.

'C'mon,' Angus said playfully, leaning forward as if to sprint. 'I'll race you.'

Sarah and Ian Og were off at once, heels kicking up dust as they jostled to be first. Angus didn't move until he found his pipe in his sporran, and stuck it unlit into his mouth. Then he led Pepper, and walked in their wake.

Close to the croft it was very still and quiet. 'It's like a graveyard here,' Angus muttered as he walked through the door.

Sarah and Ian Og were already inside, wearing shocked expressions. Dadda, Roderick and Ranald sat silent. The three youngsters were still in bed, tears mingling with occasional hiccups of sadness. It was obvious from the silent group slumped around the room that something terrible had taken place.

'Mamma,' Sarah cried out, as she ran through into the other room, where Grannie Morag was straightening out the still-warm figure. 'Mamma,' she cried again.

Dadda's eyes were bloodshot and wet, the lashes almost stuck together. When he saw Angus, he said one word – 'Mary' – and then began to sob again as he followed Sarah into the bedroom.

'Mary! My wee Mary! Don't be dead,' he threw himself down on the bed and kissed the unresponsive face, and stroked her hair.

'Come,' said Grannie Morag, drawing Sarah out of the room. 'There's work to do.' She passed her a wriggling bundle. 'Someone has to care for this motherless mite.'

In the big room, clutching her newborn brother carefully in her arms, Sarah stood still and looked around at the family. With a mighty sniff she lifted the baby towards them so they might all see the tiny crumpled face.

'It's a boy.' Sarah announced solemnly. 'We must love and look after him, and always remember that he is the last gift that Mamma left us.'

Ian Og rose from his chair beside the fire, gently steered Sarah towards it and helped her to sit down before putting crowdie, a bannock and a mug of ale laced with whisky nearby. At the same time, he filled Ranald and Roderick's mugs with whisky before drawing his younger brother to one side, and taking him out to the byre. Together they saddled a horse. Wee Anghie mounted swiftly and set off to give Father Malachy the news.

Back in the house the twins had moved to sit close to Sarah, offering their help to look after the baby, who was beginning to stir. Eileen got a bowl of fresh milk, and Wee Morag fetched a linen cloth. Sarah began to drip the milk into the hungry baby's mouth with Wee Morag's linen strip soaked in Eileen's bowl of milk.

When Ian Og came back in to the house, he got whisky and brought it to the other room for Grannie Morag, Dadda and Uncle Angus as they prayed together. Mamma lay on the bed as if asleep, and Ian Og kissed her cold forehead, before leaving the room with tears in his eyes.

There were many visitors during the following days at the croft. Mamma was laid to rest three days later. After the burial, Father Malachy baptised the newest member of the family. He was called James, after God's chosen King of Scotland. Sarah was heartened to see Cousin Alistair, but with her responsibility for young

James, already dubbed 'Wee Jimmy', she had little opportunity to chat with him.

The clansmen were keen to swap the latest news with Alistair, who was Keppoch's main courier. Hearts were already cheering in Lochaber glens, as word came that 'Bonnie Prince Charlie' was assembling many followers and regiments in France and Ireland. It would not be long before they arrived in Scotland.

The crowd slowly waned and the family talked of what value they might be to their prince, when they welcomed him and his army: Ian Og was now famed for slaying the rogue drover MacCannie, and was destined to become a mighty warrior. Alistair would never forget how his young cousin saved him from certain death when he was on his way to meet The Frenchman.

Angus Sticks' knowledge of every secret trail over mountains and glens would be invaluable. Hamish's work at the smithy beside the fort put him in an ideal position to supply vital intelligence for the cause.

As they talked through the night, they agreed that The Frenchman and other double agents and traitors must be found and stopped. They talked about MacCannie's sons, who were already terrorising towns and villages, and had sworn to get even with Alistair Glic and his clansmen. The sun was high when the last man, with a mighty thirst, sought water and laid himself down to sleep in the byre.

Next in

The Lochaber Glen Trilogy

Book 2

Five years after the events in Glen Rowan, Bonnie Prince Charlie lands in the northwest of the Scottish Highlands in 1745. The MacDonells and other clans must still deal with the daily problems of family life in Lochaber, while also joining in the Jacobite efforts to defeat the Hanoverian government, and return the Stuart dynasty to its rightful place on the throne of Scotland and England.

Release date April 2022

Book 3

The year is 1746 and 'Butcher' Cumberland's army makes its way north for a final attempt to put a stop to any further rebellion. Loyal to the Stuart cause, the Glen Rowan MacDonells make ready for battle, but are soon overwhelmed. Most clansmen return to defend their own glen, but the Glen Rowan MacDonells find a way to shield Bonnie Prince Charlie, and assist in his eventual safe departure from Scotland.

Release date October 2022

An **Audible Download** of *Glen Rowan,* read by the author, Anne L. MacDonell, is available now from:

www.lochaberglen.com